One Night

The Johnson Sisters Trilogy
Book 1
Elaine Marie

This is a work of fiction. Names, characters, places, brands, media, and incidents are either the product of the author's imagination or are used fictitiously. Any resemblance to similarly named places or persons living or deceased is unintentional.

Acknowledgments

First and foremost- To all my readers and supporters, you've waited a long time. I THANK YOU!!

Andrea Skaar Rott, you are an amazing addition and a wonderful supporter.

JA Lafrance, girl, you get me. Your encouragement and support are what make this all possible.

Stephanie Stacker (aka Stacker Designs) always provides the perfect covers and sticks by through it all. I can't thank you enough.

Last but not least, my family: Without your support and encouragement, I wouldn't have the courage to push through and bring these stories to life. Thank you for always having my back through thick and thin. I love you!

Chapter One

THE RAIN STEADILY FELL as I glanced out the window, waiting for my coffee to brew. Another week has gone by in this dead-end job of mine. Thankfully, it's Friday. Who would have thought at the age of twenty-six that I'd still be working the desk job I accepted after graduation four years ago.

The job isn't hard or worse even. It's boring as fuck. I like to stay busy. If something comes across my desk, it doesn't sit. I take it and do what needs doing. Whether I'm processing an invoice, paying a bill, or revising a contract, I get it done, and then I'm done. So, it makes for a long day, which makes for an even longer week.

I slide my arm through the cardigan and step through my kitchen doorway. The aroma of fresh Columbian coffee comes from the brewer, and I approach the counter reaching for my favorite coffee mug.

It was a gift from my sister, Nicki. With a smile, I pull the coffee pot from the hot plate and pour my morning pleasure into the mug with the dancing unicorn. The saying is written on it: With a fuck fuck here, and a fuck fuck there. Here a fuck there a fuck, everywhere a fuck fuck. She had given Keni, our youngest sister, and me them for Christmas two years ago.

I giggle at the memory of my mother's expression. Her big brown eyes almost popped out of her head. Of course, we all burst out laughing and had mom make a pot of coffee so we could break them in. I know mom wasn't offended. She was probably jealous that Nicki hadn't bought her one.

It's the little things I miss about being around family. Sitting, discussing what our plans were for the day. The smell of bacon or sausage cooking while we got ready in the mornings. Or the way Dad always walked in and kissed mom on the cheek, saying good morning before he left to build his next masterpiece.

He designed and made custom furniture out back in his makeshift shop, originally our car's garage. As he would say, no overhead means more profit. It didn't pay a lot, but we never struggled. We have always had a roof over our heads and food on our plates. It's how my parents are, not into all the material things. Not like the neighbors, well, some of them at least. Mom claims that as long as you can smile about one thing a day, it's a good life.

Living alone, in a town over from Teaneck, and working full time, we hardly see each other. My sisters and I are all at different places in our lives. I, being the most responsible and oldest, have moved out. I pay my own bills and work my ass off just to get by, even with a decent job. Who knew cable and wi-fi could be so freaking expensive? But I'm doing it, and that's something to be proud of.

I've been living off of ramen noodles and peanut butter this last month. Don't you dare tell my mom! She'd be yelling at me. I could hear her now: "you should've come over; we always have extra. Why didn't you call? Here is a couple of bucks." I actually have been saving to go out tonight and celebrate with everyone. It's my sister Keni's twenty-first birthday, and we're partying it up at the Wigwam, a quaint bar with plenty of memories.

Nicki promised to decorate the back corner and have the DJ play all of our favorite tunes. I'm sure she will end up going home with a random fling. She usually does, but that's her. "A live life in the moment," kind of gal. Sometimes I wish I could be more like her, other times- not on your life!

Mom and Dad have already texted that they will come and eat with us but were adamant about leaving prior to the shenanigans. It's my job to have fun, stay sober and keep Keni supplied with alcohol. It should be interesting, to say the least. Here I am at twenty-six and still babysitting my little sisters, though I do have to admit I am excited about celebrating another twenty-first.

After seeing the dark grey clouds glare on the screen, I check the weather app on my phone and grab the umbrella from the closet. With the door closing behind me, I slide my phone into my wristlet and listen for the lock to engage. I quickly dash between the raindrops through the small courtyard and onto the sidewalk with keys in hand. I take the stairs down to my parking lot, wiping the quick falling droplets off of my face and praying my hair doesn't get flat. The only thing worse than rain is humidity.

I click the key fob that I hold in my hand; the car chirps, and I chuck the umbrella onto the front seat floor and climb in. Once it's idling smoothly, I put it into first gear and head out. The only advantage of my job is my hours. I normally work nine to four and miss most traffic. Once in a while, I go through town and get stuck behind a school bus, but otherwise, it's a quick ten-minute trip.

Once I'm settled in at my desk, I check my emails. Three replies and two updates later, I look to my bin sitting at the corner of my desk. Lifting the few papers, I fan through the small pile. Four contracts and one maintenance agreement need to be done by the end of the day. With a glance at the clock, it's nine-thirty, and I turn my attention to the documents and open the program on my computer.

An hour and a half later, and I'm done. Ugh, now what do I do for the next five hours?

I click on the Facebook icon and scroll, adding a few books to my TBR list as I go. Since my romantic life is basically non-existent, I live vicariously through the talent of indie authors. I wish I had the courage to write and publish some of the things these authors do. I'm talking anything goes, literally. In the last two years, I may honestly say I have not read a book that didn't have a curse, a tit, a cock, or a sex scene. Yeah, these are my people.

As the phone rings, I pick it up and answer, "good morning, and thank you for calling. This is Danielle. How can I help you?" The customer requested a copy of their last lease via email. I take down the email address and the account number with my pen in hand. While he continues to talk about nothing that concerns me, I pull up my outlook. I open a new message and attach the scanned lease document with a click. By the time the guy on the other end finishes his sentence, I reply, "if you check your email, you should have it." He does, "wow, that was quick. Thank you," he says.

"No problem. If you need anything else, feel free to reply to the email or call back." We say our goodbyes, and I turn to check my reminders. My yearly physical is at four-thirty. Shit, I forgot. I should be able to get in and out without it interfering with my arrival time for the party. I set an alarm reminder for four o'clock, so I ensure I don't forget again and go back to scrolling the internet.

Chapter Two

IT'S ALMOST TIME TO get ready and go, the clock on the wall reads three forty, and I'm grateful to have the weekend in my sights. My messenger pings, alerting me that I have a new notification. I turn and face the monitor and, to my surprise, it reads:

Jacob Reynolds

Unsure if I want to open the box, I contemplate. If I reply now, we could be talking for hours. I've missed him, but now is not exactly the right time to start up a long-distance conversation. My hand shakes the mouse back and forth, and then I stop, letting it hover over the notification.

Jacob fucking Reynolds.

$$* * *$$

The Reynolds residence was a lot bigger than ours. I guess it's good to come from money. It was nestled behind the circular driveway, but we had a full view right across the street.

He climbed from the expensive-looking car, which rolled to a stop right in front of the big white doors. He looked so angry. The family had moved into the house not long into the summer before High school started. It was only three months since Lilly and Doug, Jacob's Grandparents, had passed. They were the oldest yet kindest couple in the neighborhood.

Every year since I could remember, they would cater a barbecue for the neighbors once a month. It usually started during the spring, and then they would have a huge Labor Day party weekend. The in-ground pool was open to anyone as long as they were respectful. I personally enjoyed sitting out on the patio and admiring the stone wall and flowers the gardeners planted. It was sad how they tragically passed in the car accident.

Mr. and Mrs. Reynolds, Gwyn, and Douglas, their son, and daughter-in-law, were very fancy. Definitely, upper class, as I guess his parents were. Unlike Doug, his son insisted we call him by his full name, Douglas or Mr. Reynolds. Boy, were they different. They barely spoke to any of the neighbors, never mind continuing the tradition of the barbecues. In fact, they were hardly ever here. Especially when Jacob was, which I found odd. My parents were always home for the most part.

Jacob is my age, a loner, a player, and hates how his parents treat him like an object instead of a son. He went to a live-in private school, which I thought was weird. He was hardly ever there... until he was.

Sophomore year ended, and summer had started. After a quick dip in the Reynolds pool, I lay back to take in some sun and read the newest release from my favorite author. I figure if they aren't going to be here to enjoy it, I will.

"Why don't you stay for dinner? I'm ordering pizza." Jacob walks out of the screen door and approaches the lounge I'm relaxing in. Dropping the book to the side, I grabbed the towel to cover my body. I thought he wasn't due back from school until next week. How did I not know he was home?

"You startled me." I tighten the towel. He chuckles and slides his hands into his dark blue dress pants. After I stand, he loosens his tie, and the top two buttons of his school dress shirt are being undone as I swoon over the hunk of a guy who stands before me.

Dark brown, shaggy hair hangs over his left eye. He tilts his head up and, with his hands, removes the tie altogether. Damn.

We are neighbors, friends, that's all. Besides, he's not even my type. I like a good boy who does his homework on time, goes to every class and enjoys a good book now and then.

Jacob is as bad as they come. It's why I look out for him. Someone needs to. Besides, what are best friends for? But damn, a girl can admire and appreciate puberty just as much as a boy does. He has changed from a tall skinny kid too. Let me just say it, wow! His shoulders have gotten wider, and he's filled out with muscle, and it looks good on him.

That summer went by so fast. We spent every waking moment together. You'd think we were dating. But it wasn't like that, not with us. We just... clicked. It was nice to have someone my age to talk to. Someone to hang out with and call when bored. I could tell him anything, and there was no judgment. I trusted him and appreciated that he trusted me, too.

I smile at the thought of us so young, so innocent. I turn and face the picture frame on my desk as I recall when it was taken.

It's a month before senior prom and guess who doesn't have a date? Me.

I can't believe Nicki talked me into this. I think as I walk up the brick circular driveway and knock on the white French doors of the Reynolds home. Jacob is home for the weekend. Now that he has a car, he can come and go as he pleases.

Gwyn answers, "hello Danielle, Jacob's upstairs in his room. Go ahead up." She says. I thank her and climb the wide spiral stairs slowly.

Is he going to laugh at me? Will he even consider it? My nerves cause butterflies to flutter inside my stomach to the point I feel nauseous.

I stop at the door, take a deep breath, and knock. The door opens a moment later.

"Hey Dani, come on in. I was going to call you." He sits back on his bed, throwing a book to the side. I plop down on the beanbag chair, not able to make eye contact. I can't believe I'm going to do this.

"What's up?" he slides to the edge of the bed. Keeping my face planted on the ground, I nervously look up through my eyelashes. "Dani, what's going on?" his concern grows.

"Are you going to your prom?" I ask skittishly, fidgeting with my fingers.

He grunts and slides back a little. "Hell no, that shit sucks at my school. I saw old pictures and videos online. Talk about lame as fuck." He leans down, reaches out, and ruffles my hair. "What's going on, Dani? You're normally more talkative. Something the matter?"

I take a deep breath, "Can I ask you for a favor?" He nods, so I continue, "will you come to my prom with me? I mean, as friends, of course. But I really want to go, and no one has asked." I spat out as quickly as I could. It was like pulling off a band-aide. It stung for a second.

Jacob starts to laugh, then realizes I'm serious and stops. Pushing up onto my knees, I lower my standards to beg.

"Please, Jacob. It's just one night. I promise I'll make it fun. I'll even pay for everything. Please?" I crawl closer to the bed.

He thinks for a moment, looks at me, then looks away again. After a few more "pleases," he takes my hands in his and pulls me off the ground as we stand.

"Fine, I'll go. Stop begging like a bitch. My god Dani. No one asked you, really? What a bunch of assholes." He pulls me in for a hug.

"I didn't expect to be asked. I just thought, maybe. But then the cheerleaders and popular girls made it all about them and..." I let out a tear as he held me.

"I'm sorry, D. I'd be honored to take you. But just one night, this one time, and don't be trying to show me off to all your friends." I squeeze him tighter, wrapping my arms around his neck, "thank you, Jacob, thank you so much. You are the best friend a girl could ever ask for!"

Filled with excitement, I kiss his check, unwrap my arms from his neck and run out of the house with the biggest smile on my face. Nicki was waiting at the end of the driveway, jumping up and down, clapping with Keni. "He said yes!" I grabbed both their hands, looking both ways as we crossed the street.

Prom night was amazing. Jacob insisted on getting a limo, a corsage, and he refused to accept any money, no matter how much I offered. We arrived in style, and all the cheerleaders' heads were turned in the nerd girl's direction. Unable to believe, not only did I have the nerve to intrude on their prom, but I brought the hottest guy in town.

Sure, Jacob is hot as hell, but they don't know him. They don't care that he's not happy living in a huge house. He is home alone most of the time because his parents are off on a cruise or business trip to another country. Or the fact his parents are disrespectful to him, and he's only a bad boy to piss them off.

Jacob takes my hand in his, brings it to his lips, and presses down lightly. The butterflies in my stomach settle as a smile spreads across my face from ear to ear.

"This one night is all yours. Fuck these bitches." I nod in agreement, and we walk further into the hall. He excuses himself and steps away, heading towards the DJ, whispers in his ear, and hands him a folded bill. The guy nods and then starts moving things around on his table.

Jacob returns with determination in his stride, "you ready?" My eyes go wide, not knowing what he has up his sleeve.

The song ends, and a familiar beat sounds through the speakers. An oldie but goodie, Cherry Pie by Warrant. It's the song we joke about because my parents are still living in the eighties and nineties, yet we have come to enjoy it, too. As he leads me to the middle of the dance floor, my cheeks flush as I scan the room, and all eyes are on us.

He draws my attention back to him, "Dani, fuck them. You're here with me. Besides, you promised me a good time." I take a deep breath; he starts dancing, and I follow suit.

I never laughed, danced, or had so much fun. The night came to an end, and Jacob, being the gentleman he is, walked me to my door.

"I really had a good time tonight." He takes my hand in his. "Me too, oh my god, I would have hated being there with anyone else. Thank you." I lean in to kiss him on the cheek. Instead, he turns, and our lips touch. I pause for a moment, shocked, until his arm wraps around my hip and his other cradles my neck pulling me closer.

Not expecting this, I gasp, and he takes full advantage. His tongue touches mine, and my eyes pop open. He pulls back slightly, asking permission with his eyes.

"I've never. I mean..." I admit in a whisper but want more. Without any more hesitation, I place my hand behind his neck and tug him down for another kiss.

After a moment, we both pull away. He tucks his hands into his pockets and looks up and down the block, avoiding all eye contact.

Breaking the silence and awkwardness, I tell him, "It was a hell of a night. Thanks, Jacob." I turn on my heels with a smile and reach out for the knob, escaping through my front door.

"Night, Cherry Pie," he says as the door closes, and I can't help the giggle that escapes.

I look at the messenger box with his name again. It's been a while since we've spoken, and it would be good to catch up. I'm glad he is keeping himself safe.

I click accept.

Jacob: Hi Dani, long time. I'm in town. Did you want to catch up?

I click reply.

Danielle: Absolutely! Wigwam tonight? It's Keni's birthday!

An immediate response pops up before I even get a chance to click the little x in the corner to close out the messenger box.

Jacob: See you there!

Chapter Three

IT'S ALMOST SIX-THIRTY, according to the watch on my wrist. I yank the heavy wood door open, and the stale smell of beer invades my nostrils. I push past the curtain. To my right is the jukebox, the bar stools, and the dark long backward three-shaped countertop lines the wall. Mirrors hang behind shelves filled with top-notch liquor bottles. I take a few steps in and place my wristlet on the tall round table against the pony wall, which divides the booths from the bar area.

The dartboard hangs just to the right of the bay window and the flickering neon Bud Light sign. A small dance floor leads to the back tables. I notice the balloons floating in the back corner with a quick glance over my shoulder. Thank God! I thought Nicki was going to forget.

"Hey Dani," Diesel walks by and heads behind the bar with extra streamers in hand. He's worked here for a few years now, along with Nicki. They, as Nicolette would say, are friends with benefits. No strings attached. Fuck Buddies, and not bad on the eye, rough and tough-looking with his muscular build. Yet a total sweetheart.

"Tell me Nicki helped at least?" I ask with a groan of guilt. I know damn well she can get a man to crawl on his knees if she wants to. He looks over his shoulder and smiles. "Actually, she did. I'm just cleaning up." He throws the bar rag down, grabs a beer from the cooler, and places it in front of one of the regulars in the corner.

"Can I get you something?" He places a coaster on the bar, and I step closer. "Um…" I glance at my watch. What the hell? After the unexpected news I just got from my doctor, I could use a drink. I'll have one or two then eat, so I'm sober to get everyone home later.

"Sex on the Beach, please." He smirks, nods, and turns to make it. I lean over and grab a cherry from the plastic container sitting on the edge with my elbows on the bar.

"Now that sounds like fun," a deep voice comes from behind. I roll my eyes and ignore the rude comment. Maybe the idiot isn't even talking to me.

"With you, it would probably be amazing." I feel someone behind me, a little too close for my comfort. I glance up to see the reflection in the mirror, but the bottles block it. Diesel's eyes are large with surprise. I know he'll have my back if I need him. But he knows we Johnson's sisters can take care of ourselves.

After the boring day at work and the doctor telling me there is a lump I need to have checked, I'm not in the mood for this shit. As I start to turn to tell this guy to fuck off, I'm pressed into the bar from behind and caged in by two strong, tanned arms.

About to lose my shit, I jerk my head to look over my shoulder.

"Jacob," escapes my lips, more breathless than expected. I'm frozen in time as his taut, hard body presses against mine. His calloused fingers wrap around my wrist and spin me around. Finally, realizing this is really happening, I scream, "Jacob!" and throw my arms around his neck. My god, he looks amazing, his hair is growing back in, and I hadn't realized how much I missed him.

He kisses my cheek, and we hug for a few moments. Diesel places my drink on the bar and reaches over in greeting, "Hey, welcome back, man." I move to his side so he can shake hands.

"Good to be back." He says, grabs my drink, and leads us to the round table nestled against the wall.

"It's so good to see you. How long has it been?" I ask, knowing damn well it's been ten months and four days since I dropped him at the airport to report back to duty.

Jacob turned eighteen and, to piss off his parents, decided that he would join the Army rather than going to college and working for the family.

"Almost a year, he says." Lifts his hand and pushes the long strands of hair behind my ear. "You look good," he withdraws, and I swat at him, giggling like a little school girl.

"So do you, I see, letting your hair grow again." I tousle it back and forth. He leans back out of reach. I admire this grown man sitting before me, a moment of silence passes. The front door and curtain swing open, and Nicki walks in. In her black ripped jeans and tank top, she never fails to amaze me. She has dyed her hair jet black, too. The blood-red lipstick matches her nails and shoes. When she turns in our direction, she waves, and smiles.

"Still hell on heels, I see," Jacob says and stands in greeting. She sashays her ass over and plants a kiss right on his lips. I take a deep breath. It's fine.

"Welcome home, soldier!" She looks over her shoulder. "Hey Diesel, anything they want, it's on me." I look to see his reaction. Jealousy is a bitch. I see his stare toward Jacob when Nicki snakes her arm around his neck. I guess we have that in common. Not that either one of us has claimed or admitted our attractions out loud. But I've seen the signs. Diesel's got it bad for Nicki. He shakes his head and walks to the far side of the bar.

"How ya been, little sister?" Jacob sits back down on the high stool. "You know me, all good." She glances around the bar, scoping out her next victim, I'm sure.

"Nicki, what time are Mom and Dad bringing Keni?" She grabs my arm and glances at my watch.

"They should be here any minute. Come on in the back. Kendra's friends are already here." She rolls her eyes, with a tilt of her head, in the direction of the buffet table.

The black and gold sparkle signs hang from the ceiling, and wall-to-wall pink and blue streamers with matching balloons.

"It looks great, Nicki. You did a really good job." I admit, surprised.

"Actually, Kendra's friends did most of it before I even got here." she shrugs her shoulders. "Diesel and I hung the signs, and the girls did the streamers."

'Lookout, I'm legal', '21 and able', 'If you can read this, pick me up': a few silly sayings are hanging in the dining area.

As I glance around the few tables designated for our group, I think maybe I should have rented a minibus.

"So, what's the plan?" After seeing the empty bottles on the table, Jacob looks at me with wide eyes.

I chuckle, "Watch them drink until they puke, and then drive them home." He shakes his head, "Seriously? Ah, to be twenty-one again." I can't help the laugh, which escapes a little louder than expected.

With a nod, I motion to a secluded table. Apart from the younger crew, he follows with a smile.

Once we are seated, I listen to the music and feel his eyes on me.

"What?" I question why he is sitting and staring in my direction.

"Nothing. I guess I didn't realize how much I missed you." He takes the bottle of beer to his lips. "I'm so glad you're here." I take my glass and hold it up in salute, then sip. The girls to the right of us stand and start cheering. Looking over Jacob's shoulder, I see the light come through the doorway.

Kendra walks in, raises her arms, and yells, "let's drink bitches!" Screeching echoes throughout the room.

My parents scan the table of booze and send each other a silent message. When they turn, they notice us, off to the side in the corner, and make quick use to escape the craziness that has begun.

Immediately, Jacob stands and sticks out his hand, "Good evening David, Julie. Nice to see you again." My father takes his hand, shakes then pulls him in for a hug. Mom follows suit and does the same. "Welcome home, son."

They have always welcomed Jacob into our home, on vacation trips, just about everything for as many years as I can remember. I guess he's the son they never had. Don't get me wrong, the three of us girls have given them both good and bad times throughout the years. But having a son would have been a blessing. It wasn't in the cards. After mom had Keni, she had to have a partial hysterectomy.

My parents join us at the adult table as we make faces and shiver, recalling the taste of Jägermeister when the girls pound shots in celebration of my baby sister's birthday. The food is brought out, and we all fill up on chicken wings, potato skins, penne in vodka sauce, chicken francese, and teriyaki beef. While waiting to fill my plate, my mom asked the question that I was dreading.

"How was your appointment, all good?" I turn slowly, "I have to go for testing." She stops, puts her plate down, and squares off with me. "Danielle, what's wrong?" I shake my head, "not here, Mom, not tonight. Okay?" I plead, and with those few words, she knows and pulls me in for a hug. I swallow hard, keeping my fear in check.

We separate, trying not to draw attention and fill our plates. Once we have what we want, we head back to the table. Small talk between my parents and Jacob fills the time while I enjoy another drink. The food is delicious, and since it's been a rough day, I decided to have another. By the looks of these girls, we aren't leaving anytime soon. I see it's almost nine with a quick glance at my wrist. Mark takes over at the bar, and Diesel and Nicki join us.

"Shots all around," Nicki places a tray in the middle of the girls' table as Diesel approaches ours. I shake him off, "Nope, I'm done drinking. I'm in charge of getting all these drunks home."

"Bummer," he says and offers the drinks to my parents. They deny and excuse themselves, ready to take their leave. Dad leans in, kisses my cheek, and says, "If you need a hand getting them home, call." I nod and stand to hug Mom. She whispers, "everything will be okay. I'm here for you. Just a phone call away." With that, she kisses my cheek, saying goodnight.

They wave their goodbyes from the door, and the DJ stops the music. Keni, Jillian, and Erika jump up and make their way to the small, square dance floor. Nicki comes over, grabs my hand, and pulls me out to have some fun with my sisters.

"Ladies and gentlemen, let's give it up for the Johnson sisters. Dani and Nicki would like you all to join in celebrating their baby sister, Keni's, birthday! Let's all toast: Happy twenty-first, Kendra!" Every patron in the bar claps and starts to sing. Keni is so embarrassed, and I love it. Jacob comes over, picks her up in a bear hug, whispers something in her ear, and she laughs.

After a few songs, I find myself more interested in the conversation being held at the table between Jacob and Diesel. I maneuver my way through the small crowd of girls dancing and wonder if I was ever this carefree. Being an adult sucks!

Mark walks over with a large glass of water with lemon, exactly what I need. I thank him and feel Jacob's eyes on me. I collapse into the chair in relief of my sore feet.

Thankfully, the music isn't too loud back here. "I'm too old for this shit," I complain, pulling at my shirt to air out. Beads of sweat line my hairline. Jacob picks up a napkin and wipes my forehead, proceeding to reach for my glass of water with lemon. He places it in front of me, sits back, and rests his arm against the back of my stool, sliding me closer.

"It's good to see you out and having fun because you were all about work last time I was home," he says, and I shrug my shoulders. "So, how long are you home for? Where are you staying?" I ask, hoping we can make plans for the time he's here.

"Actually, I was just telling Diesel I'm home for good." My eyes must have been as wide as saucers, disbelief written on my face.

Nicki comes over, "Dani, what's wrong?" I ignore her and turn to stare into Jacob's eyes, absorbing what he's said.

"Home, for good?" I can feel the tears begin to build. "I'm done, Danielle. I'm home." I jump from the stool and into his lap without even thinking. All the worry, the sleepless nights wondering if he was okay, if he was coming back. Don't get me wrong, I'm proud of him and his choice to join, but he took another piece of my heart with him every time he had to report back.

"Yes! Finally!!" Nicki pumps her fist in the air, turning to motion for Keni to come over. With only a few stumbles, she makes it to the table. "What's up?" she asks. Nicki motions in our direction.

"Did you two finally hook up?" She says, slurring her words. "No!" we say in unison, with equal expressions of slight embarrassment flooding our faces.

Nicki snaps her fingers and gets Keni's attention, "He's done. He's home for good."

She throws her arms up in the air, her drink spilling everywhere, "welcome home, big brother. Best birthday gift ever!!!"

I appreciate how much and what a big part of our family Jacob has become over the years. But it makes me wonder, does he only see us as sisters? Hmm... kind of bums me out. I sit back on my own stool and wait for all the commotion to calm down.

I mean, we did kiss that one time after Prom, but since then, we've only been friends.

Nicki whispers something to Diesel, and he glances in my direction. They disappear from the table. It's just Jacob, and I left.

"Where will you be staying?" I ask, wiping the condensation off the side of my glass. "I have a room at the hotel. I am not going back to that house, not if my life depended on it." He states adamantly.

"I have a pull-out couch if you want to stay with me. Save some money until you find your own place." I offer without even thinking.

"Really? I wouldn't want to get in the way of your love life." I roll my eyes. What love life? "Jacob, we are friends, best friends, to be exact. What kind of person would I be if I didn't offer? Besides, if I was involved with someone, they would have to understand and accept that you are part of it." He leans over and kisses my cheek. "I love you, and I'm going to take you up on the offer. Thanks."

We sit listening to the music, and I listen as he talks about his time serving. He and his buddies would engage in the shenanigans during their downtime. As Nicki waves her arms in the air, I'm distracted frantically. I jump from the table. Jacob immediately follows as we make it halfway to the dance floor. We witness Nicki and Keni holding her friend, Jillian, and they, rushing past us toward the bathroom.

"Looks like the party's over," I say and follow them in.

Once she pukes, and we get her cleaned up, Kendra admits she is done. Thank God for the wall, or she'd be on the floor. I glance at my watch, "all good, kiddo, it's almost closing time.

Did you have fun?" She nods and stumbles to the door. When she yanks it open, Jacob is there to catch her.

"I have Diesel bringing your car around," he says, and I'm grateful I don't have to do this alone.

We make our way through the bar and grab Erika. When we step outside, the cool air is refreshing. Nicki follows us out, "I'm going to stay to help clean up and close out. You sure you can drive everyone home?" she asks. "Yeah, thanks for tonight." I step over and wrap her in my arms. She may be the wild and crazy one, but she will always have our backs when it comes to family and friends.

Jacob helps me put the girls in my car. "I'll follow you. Make sure you don't need help." I giggle, "Thanks, two stops. Erika and Jillian are in the dorms on River Road, then Keni is going home." He nods, gets in the rental car, and parks a few spots up.

With a glance in the side-view mirror, I make sure no one is coming and pull out onto Cedar Lane.

Thirty minutes later, I am parked in front of my parents' house, and Kendra is passed out drunk in the back seat. With my cell phone, I snap a few photos so I can break her chops at a later date.

Once I have enough, I get out and lean against the passenger door. Jacob is parked behind me, and I hear him exit and walk over to join me. We talk for a little while, giving Keni some time to wake up. "I'll come to the apartment tomorrow then," and I nod my head in agreement. Suddenly, the back door swings open, and Kendra pukes on the side, against the curb. Gross.

"Well, at least she didn't puke in the car." Jacob chuckles as he holds the door for her.

"Come on, kiddo." I grab some tissues from the box on my front seat and wipe her face the best I can. I swing one arm around her and Jacob and guide her up the small path to the door. My dad opens it as we approach as if he's been waiting for this moment. He snaps a photo and quickly tosses his phone onto the table to the side.

"Blackmail," he wiggles his eyebrows. I laugh, "I did the same." My arm slides down her back, trying to steady her on her own two feet. She sways back and forth.

"To be young again," Dad says and slides his arm around her, then under her legs, cradling Keni like he did when she was a little girl. "I love you, Daddy," she says, and her head falls back.

"Thanks, Dad, night. Love you, talk to you tomorrow." He blows me a kiss and retreats into the house. I close the door and lock it up for him.

Jacob and I say our goodnights, and I thank him for his assistance. "I'm glad you're back, see you tomorrow!" I close my car door and head home.

Once inside, I cozy up on the couch, turn the TV on and fall asleep before I even decide what to watch.

Yeah, to be young again.

Jacob

It was bittersweet holding Dani in my arms again. David and Julie are always so kind. It was good to have dinner with them all. Diesel offered some hours at the bar until I could find better work, which would help me get my own place. The elevator door opens on the third floor, and I follow the worn-down carpet to my room, slide the key in, and the green lights flash.

Once the door is closed and I'm inside, I glide the chain on, kick off my boots, unbutton my jeans and pull my shirt over my head.

I lie back and turn the TV on, grab my phone and pull up my photo album.

My favorite picture stares back at me. Dani and I were standing outside in the sun, she in her bikini and I in my long shorts. Her smile was so big as she laughed at something stupid I said. It was so natural, so innocent, and so beautiful. It's when I think I realized I loved her. Not like a sister, not like Nicki or Keni.

No, there was definitely something between us. I felt it on Prom night when we kissed. So, when she started seeing that dickhead Jarred, I knew I couldn't stay around and watch. The next week I went for my physical and officially joined the military.

It hurt so much seeing her spend time with another, almost as bad as getting shot in my shoulder. I unknowingly rub the scar.

With a yawn, I grab the pillow, tuck it under my arm, close my eyes and willingly fall asleep.

Chapter Four

UP BRIGHT AND EARLY, I run down Queen Anne Road making my way back to the hotel. My mornings are routine. After I took the bullet, my commanding officer and I spoke of reenlisting. My tour was coming to an end, and I felt I was ready to come home. He shook my hand and wished me well. Once the doctors released me, I was sent back here to the states to continue with therapy.

Now, I'm back one hundred percent with an honorable discharge. Other than the scar and the memories of a late-night attack, I am as close to my old self as I ever will be. My pace picks up as I turn left down DeGraw, about a mile left before I reach the hotel.

Once inside, I make quick progress getting my things shoved into my bag. While I wait to leave for Danielle's, I take a shower to calm down. Who would have thought I'd be nervous. We are best of friends. It's not like we've never slept at each other's house. Shit, I would join them on their family vacations, for crying out loud.

I glance at the clock. It's not even nine yet, but fuck it. I lace up my boots and grab my bag. When I walk past the main entrance, the key card lands on the desk, and I head out.

It takes about twenty minutes for me to walk to Dani's. I glance up at the big bay window and see her bopping around with a gray shirt hanging off her shoulder. Her long brown hair is tossed to one side, leaving her neck exposed as she moves back and forth.

In a few quick strides, I reach door 2B and knock, but there's no answer. Knowing Dani used to leave a spare in the fake plant next to the stairs, I take the chance and reach in, and it only takes a moment to retrieve it. As quietly as possible, I unlock the door, turn the knob and push it open. I can't help the smile as I witness her goofy self-dancing while she mops the wood floor.

..*

Danielle

With the earbuds playing one of my favorite songs, I stop and admire the cleanliness of the floor. After my first cup of coffee, I rushed to get the place clean in anticipation of Jacob's arrival. I can't believe I asked him to stay with me. With a shimmy to the left and then to the right, I turn and "Holy fuck!" I drop the Swiffer and grab it at my chest.

"You scared the shit out of me!" I pull the earbuds out and take a few deep breaths.

"I'm sorry, I didn't mean to," he says with a chuckle.

I wave him off and step towards the kitchenette, "Coffee?"

"No, I'm good. Thanks." He sits and waits as I make my last cup.

"How'd you sleep?" I wonder while pouring my cream and sugar into the mug.

"You know me, same as usual," he shrugs. And I do know him. I pull the chair out and sit, placing the coffee on the table with a smile. "Hey, remember when we were kids, and you would call me at like two in the morning, asking me to come out. I'd sneak over, and we'd sit in the backyard staring up at the stars. I miss that. Being young, I mean, with no cares in the world." I sip, and the side of his mouth twitches.

"Why did we ever say, I can't wait to grow up?" He fiddles with his cell phone, spinning it in circles. Then asks, "Any plans? I mean, should I know anything?" I tilt my head to the side, not knowing what exactly he is asking.

He waves his arms in the air, motioning around the apartment, "in regards to staying here, like don't come in if there is a sock on the door." He glances around, but not in my direction, as if he is dreading the answer.

"No, I'll leave a tie. Socks are just gross- feet yuck!" I tell him with a little shiver in my shoulders.

"Why would you have a tie?" He leans back and crosses his legs.

With a wink, I grab my cup and stand. "Wouldn't you like to know?" I smirk, take a few steps to pick up the mop, walk it into the closet and close the door. With a turn, I step towards the counter, and to keep myself occupied, I wipe it down, trying not to avoid his stare. Was that disappointment I saw?

"Make yourself at home. I have to run to the store for a few things. Add anything you need or want to the list. First, I'm going to take a shower." I toss a pen and paper onto the table, lean back against the fridge door, and cross my arms. He nods, and I excuse myself.

Talk about the house getting really cold, real fast.
So what if I own a tie. I mean, lots of girls do, right?

Chapter Five

Jacob

I NEED TO GO DO SOMETHING. I can't sit here while she is on the other side of the wall, all wet and ugh, and a tie. She owns a tie? What has my little innocent Danielle been up to all these years? What has she not been telling me? Forget it. I let my mind wander into dangerous territories. The dreams I have of her, could she be doing all those things with someone else?

Do I really want to know?

I grab the pen from the counter and leave a note.

Be back later. I took the spare key.

I close the door behind me and feel anger building inside. Suddenly I want to hit something or someone.

No, I do not want to know.

I pull my cell from my pocket and hit Diesel with a text: You up?

Crossing the street, I find comfort in the warm sun. Before I know it, I'm climbing the steps and banging on Diesel's front door.

The door pry's open slowly, and to my surprise, Nicki is standing there in Diesel's shirt and nothing else but panties. She runs her fingers through her hair as if I've awakened her.

"Why in the loving fucking hell are you banging on the door so early in the morning?" Forgetting they work late hours, I apologize. I wasn't thinking at all. My mind was all over the place, stuck on Dani. Doing the nasty, using a tie while some jerk touched her soft skin. I shake my head.

"Sorry, I didn't realize you and Diesel were a thing." She waves me off and retreats into his apartment.

"We're not." She grabs her pants and slides them on. Diesel stumbles out of the bathroom.

"What's up, bro?" He rubs his hand over his face.

"Nothing, I obviously interrupted. I'll go. I'll swing by later." I grab the door handle and escape the uncomfortable feeling of seeing my little sister half-naked. And what is she thinking, fucking Diesel?

Don't get me wrong, he is a great guy, but he always came across as a one-woman man.

Nicki is in no way ready to put down roots. She is the biggest party animal I know. Shit, she can drink half my squad under the table, and I think she fucked the other half when we came here on leave last year.

The guys used to bust my chops because I wouldn't want to hear the stories of their wild time with someone I consider a sister. But as they say, she was an adult, and she was who came onto them. So I should stay out of it.

With nowhere else to go, I find myself wandering the streets. Without realizing I find myself standing at the end of the driveway of my parent's home. I don't miss this place at all.

A mistake is what they called me more often than not. It's why I was sent away to school. It's why in the summers when I was home, they made plans and business trips, so they weren't. And it is exactly why when dear old dad told me to join the family business or get out, I packed up and left. Never looking back.

I cross over and knock on Johnson's door.

"Good morning David," I greet the man I consider more of a father than the business suit who paid to keep me out of his hair.

"Morning, son," he says, and we make our way into the kitchen to find Julie making sandwiches. It's late morning, and they already have the oldies station on the radio. Recalling all the days when we were kids, I'd come in, and they would be dancing around the room.

I kiss her on the cheek and find a seat at the table, "so, has the birthday girl made it out of bed yet?"

They throw each other a glance, and Julie turns, placing a plate down for David.

"Welp, she threw up three more times after she got here. Then proceeded to pass out on the stairs." She rolls her eyes.

"Lightweight," I chime in, and we laugh. With that, a shuffling noise comes from the doorway.

"Mom, Aleve, please. For fucks sake, can you lower the damn radio?" She is a complete mess. Hair in every direction possible, her mascara smeared to the point she looks like a raccoon. I quickly pull my phone and snap a picture.

"Keni, how about a nice juicy –" She throws her hands up over her ears and narrows her eyes. Giving me the death glare, stopping my next words.

"Jacob, I love you. But for the love of God, if you finish that sentence, I will have to kill you." She plops down on the chair and places her head against her arms.

"I know what you really need." I begin, "Taylor ham, egg, and cheese."

Her head slowly lifts, "that does sound good."

"Mm, hmm. But I'm not going anywhere with you looking like that." I nod, dismissing her to clean up. She pushes herself off the table, "give me ten, and you're driving." I smile. She probably woke up still feeling tipsy.

"You are so good to my girls. I'm glad they have you." David lifts his glass of soda, and with a smile, he drinks.

"I'm the lucky one." These people are my family. My best friend, my two little sisters, and my parents don't mind spending time with you.

Chapter Six

AFTER KENI ATE AND insisted we get milkshakes, she wasn't ready to go home yet.

"Jacob, you need a car. How much can you spend?" she asked, then sipped from the straw. Well, my account has money, but I rather not spend much. "My earnings are slim, and I have to find a place to live. I can't stay on your sister's couch forever."

She laughs out loud, "you're sleeping on her couch?" We stop at the red light, and I turn to face her, "Uh yeah, why?" She nods and opens the window.

"You two are a joke. One day you'll both wake up." She leans back, closes her eyes, and enjoys the wind on her face as we make our way through town. We pull up to the used car lot on the edge of town.

I put the car in park, and we exit. I walk up to an apple red Packard, in mint condition, and all I can think, as I run my finger along the length of it, is I need this car.

"OMG- that's the car from the fucking video!" Keni yells, jumping up and down with excitement. I guess she is feeling better now that she has some food in her stomach.

"Yes, it is," the salesman walks over and introduces himself, "I'm Mack, welcome. Can I help you find something?" He says Kendra quickly starts fixing herself as if she's a little nervous.

I reach out and shake his hand, "Jacob, how much for her?" He walks around and gives me the rundown.

"It's a beautiful, mint condition. I rebuilt it myself. I'd hate to see it go, but you look like you appreciate her value." His eyes never leave Keni's direction, and she blushes.

"You are talking about the car, right? Because this is my sister." His head turns in my direction, "nice to know." Stepping over to the car, he leans in and starts the engine. It's like music to my ears.

"How much?" I ask again, a little giddy with excitement. I know my funds are low, but the trust fund my grandmother left for me has never been touched, and I want this car.

"Let's go inside, and we can talk." He leads us through the repair garage into an office, where Keni sits with her back straight and chest out. Mack excuses himself to retrieve paperwork.

"What the fuck, Keni? Put them away." I say, snapping my head in another direction. I do not want to witness her flirting. It's just, no! First Nicki at Diesel's, now Keni. I rub my fingers over my face and try to dismiss the images. My little sisters aren't so little anymore.

"Fine, I'll go back to my car. Are you really going to buy it? Mom and dad are going to flip," she squeals, clapping her hands and skipping out the door. I can't help the smile and excitement building.

An hour later, I texted Dani and Nicki to meet us at the Johnson family home for a barbecue, my treat. After setting the plan in motion, I sent Keni home and drove down to the local supermarket with the convertible.

I throw burgers, dogs, chicken, some rolls, and side salads in my cart.

Kendra text: Everyone's here.

I reply: Be there in ten.

Once I make it across town, I push in my music tape, and Cherry Pie starts blaring from the speakers. I park the car in front, and Julie and David rush from the front door as Dani, Nicki, and Keni come from the side of the house where the cornhole is set up.

I get out, round the car, cross my legs, and land against the passenger door.

"Holy fuck!" Dani runs up to the car. Seeing her excited makes the price tag worthwhile. Julie and David start dancing to the song on the front lawn, and we all have a good laugh.

*** ∴

Danielle

"You did not buy this car!" my eyes go wide with disbelief as I stop short to admire the beauty. "I did," Jacob answers with a grin from ear to ear.

When the song ends, he turns the car off, and I help grab the bags, and we make our way to the backyard.

"What made you buy it?" His smile is contagious. "When I saw the candy apple red car, I had to. It brought back all our summer memories. Cherry Pie was there waiting for me." He says.

"Geez, it seems like all the girls in your life do a lot of waiting," Nicki mumbles just loud enough for us to hear. What the fuck is she talking about? I ignore her, and Dad starts the grill.

Jacob explains, "I figure we can take her to the car shows this summer. I'll pick up a beater to get around town, but when I saw her, I just knew I needed to have her."

When Dad walks down, we all reach in and grab our portions while salads are passed around the table.

"That sounds like fun. Remember when we used to go on the weekends. Some of those cars were amazing." I scoop some coleslaw and plop it on Jacob's plate. He smiles, turns, grabs the mustard, and squeezes it onto my hotdog.

We enjoy dinner with the oldies rock station on, laughing and talking about old times when we were kids playing street hockey and taking family vacations down the shore. After helping mom clean up, Jacob insists we take advantage of the warm night air. "Leave your car here, and let's take a ride." Who am I to turn him down? It's not like I have any other plans.

With the wind in my hair and the radio playing our favorite classics, we hit route eighty and took off to the west. It's a smooth ride, with no traffic, and once we get up by exit nineteen, I know exactly where he is taking us.

"The gap?" I throw my hands up in the air and suck in the mountain air. It's crazy how, only an hour away, things can be so different.

The sunset begins to set, and the dark sky takes form by the time we pull up to the water's edge. The Delaware Water Gap has always been our way to get out of town and find a peaceful place. We sit quietly and listen to the water, look up to the stars and let our minds forget our worries.

"So, what are your plans now that you're home?" I ask, breaking the silence.

"I guess I'll find a job, get a girl, and settle down." He shrugs his shoulders, not even attempting to make eye contact.

"Wow, big plans." I focus on my nails, chipping away some of the week-old paint. How I wish he didn't see me as a sister. I really need to get over this fixation I've had on him for all these years.

"Dani, can I ask a favor?" He turns in my direction. "Of course? Can't say I will say yes. But you can ask." I raise my leg, bend it onto the bench seat and face him.

"Remember all the times you asked me for one night, just one time?" I nod, recalling all the favors he has done for me. There was prom night, the night I needed an escort to a college function. Oh, and who can forget my parents' thirty-year anniversary party. Whelp, I really can't count that one. I just begged him to make sure he could take leave.

"Will you come with me? I need to appear at a family wedding. My cousin. Remember Jonathan?" I nod, recalling the sexy blonde who would come for a week during the summer.

"He's your mother's brother's kid, right? Like a year younger than us?" I question, and he confirms.

"Yeah, he and Michael are getting married. My parents will be there, and I really don't want to go alone."

I consider it an excuse to get away for a weekend. Get dressed up and have some fun. Why not?

"Where and when, I got your back, just like you've always had mine. We're BFFs. It's what we do!" I shrug my shoulders, and relief moves over his face.

"Two weeks, it's a Saturday midday wedding, reception to follow in the evening. But there's a catch. It's a booze cruise wedding. So we are stuck on the ship until late Sunday after the family brunch." He laughs.

"Sounds like a dangerously good time." I giggle. We can have a blast and not worry about driving.

He starts the engine, the lights come on, and he reverses out of the spot. "I appreciate it. Let's get home. You have work in the morning." Hearing the words as simple as let's get home sends a shiver up my spine. Shaking the feeling off, he pulls out onto the highway, and an hour later, we are pulling into the apartment parking lot. My car is backed in and parked in my assigned spot, to my surprise.

"How did-" He winks, "Nicki and Keni."

God, I love my sisters.

* * *

A week later, I'm running late. I should have been out of the office fifteen minutes ago. I would have been if I hadn't answered the damn phone with only a minute to go. Ever since Jacob moved in, I have been eager to get home. We have been staying up late watching movies or just enjoying each other's company. It's as if time hasn't passed by. He makes me feel like the teenager I was, sneaking out of the house and hanging out with him. We have laughed, cried, and everything in between.

I pull into my spot and grab the pizza I picked up on the way. When I get to the door, I unlock it and rush in, having to pee. When I rush through the small apartment, I expect Jacob to be seated at the table waiting. But he's not.

I hear the water running with the pizza safely in the oven to keep warm. Shit, he's in the shower. I cross my legs, oh for fuck sake! I can't wait. I turn the knob and open the door slightly. His reflection in the mirror reveals he is washing his hair. I tiptoe in, figuring I can get in pee, and get out before he even knows.

In a rush, I squat on the toilet and let loose. With a quick wipe, I decide I'll wash my hands in the kitchen so as not to get caught. I hear the curtain pull back once my pants are up and zippered.

Wide-eyed, I look at his face and instinctively at his cock. "Hot Damn!" escapes on its own accord.

"Dani, what the fuck?" He yanks at the curtain to cover, shocked to see me standing there. I can't help the giggle, "sorry had to pee." I shrug my shoulders and step closer. I pull the curtain from his hip with my pointer finger and look down, "you have no reason to hide, be proud." He bat's my hand away. "Dani!" I shrug and wink.

"Oh really?" He drops the curtain, and I rush from the room with a full burst of laughter. "Jacob, don't you dare." I slam the door behind me.

He steps from the bathroom a moment later, wrapped in a towel.

"Hope you got a good look." He says, grabbing the t-shirt from the back of the recliner. I cross my legs and sit on the couch. "I did. I must say, I'm impressed." He looks over his shoulder, and the towel drops showing his fine-toned ass. He clenches and then proceeds to pull up his boxers as I turn my attention to the slice of pepperoni pizza in hand.

"Dani, you can drive a man crazy, you know?" He plops down beside me, leans in, and chews off a piece of the crust.

"It's fun, besides. It's not like we could ever be a couple, right?" I asked in a joking manner. Because in all reality, I think we would make a great couple. We both like all the same things, yet we give each other a hard time about certain things. Oh, hell. I am not going down this road again. I shake the thoughts from my head and place my attention on the remote in search of something to watch.

"Do you want a soda or beer?" He gets up and walks over to the kitchen. I love how he is so relaxed here with me. It's as if we were meant to be together. He's the thread to my needle. I'm his Bonnie to his Clyde. We just...are good for each other.

"Beer me!" I tell him with a smile. He gets his slice and steals the remote from my hand when he returns.

"My night to pick." He claims, and I'm okay with it.

Chapter Seven

A *week later...*

AFTER TAKING A LONG hot shower, a loud bang comes from the door. I jumped in place, startled.

"Hey, are you going to save some hot water for me?" Jacob asks. I giggle, turn the water off, and grab the towel from the counter. Quickly, I wrap it around myself and open the door.

"You should have joined me, conserve water, save the planet and all." I laugh as his eyes go wide, but he doesn't move. A surprised expression, to say the very least.

"I'm kidding, Jacob, relax. I know you don't see me that way." I place my hand on his shoulder as I walk past him and into my room, closing the door behind me.

What is with him lately? He's so damn jumpy.

* * *

Jacob

Join her? For the love of God, I did everything in my power not to sneak in and seduce her. I listened to her singing as she washed her hair, and I had to wonder what the hell took so long! And she has the nerve to joke about it? This is killing me!

I stare at myself through the mirror. It's time I start seriously looking for my own place.

With a few deep breaths, I calm myself. I've got to get a handle on this, or it's going to be a long night. I'm happy for Jonathan and Michael, but having to see my parents is going to be a kick in the face. I can see it coming.

Thank god I have Dani; she is my rock. She knows just when to be brutal and when to be sweet. After all these years, I've learned not to take her or our friendship for granted. She has gotten me through some rough times. Don't get me wrong. She has also torn out my heart and spit on it, but what she doesn't know won't hurt her, right?

As the water cascades down my body, I think about how this night is going to go. We'll have a few drinks and have our own fun as we did for her prom. We'll congratulate Jonathan and Michael and then tend to our assigned table, have some drinks, and dance the night away. Just her and I, fuck everyone else who will be there. We will have fun! I'll make sure of it.

Pleased with my plan, I turn the water off, grab a towel and go in search of my suit. Dani was nice enough to make room in the hall closet for some of my things.

Standing by the couch, I pull up my boxers and finish drying my hair. I should have gotten a haircut because the top is getting way too long.

Once I have my slacks on and am finished buttoning up my shirt, I hear the bedroom door open. Oh, for fucks sake! She steps out, leans her right arm against the door frame, and lets me take it all in.

*** *

Danielle

With my hair and makeup completed, I glance in the full-length mirror. Appreciating how Nicki's dress actually fits and looks good. I was surprised when we were hanging out the other night. She offered it to me. She claims it's her lucky dress, and I'm not sure if I want to know any more about that subject. Other than that, it just came back from the cleaners.

It's tight but breathable. The crisscross halter-style top is secure and holds my girls. As I admire the teal color, I turn and confirm the backless bodycon sequin dress is not completely zippered. I push my hair back over my shoulders and open the door. My calves look awesome in the new high heels I bought.

I grab the black and teal tie I also purchased and pull open the door. In one step, I place my right hand over my head against the door frame, place the tie, and place the other hand on my left hip, waiting for Jacob to notice I've joined him. He stops short of buttoning his top button. His eyes zero in on the bare cleavage exposed, and his jaw drops.

"I'll take that as a compliment," I say and walk in his direction. I finish buttoning his shirt and slide the tie over his head. We match perfectly. With a turn, I glance over my shoulder, "would you mind?" He follows the fabric down to my lower back with shaky hands and finishes zippering it for me. "Thanks!"

I step away and grab my wristlet.

"Umm, Dani, where is the rest of the dress?" I let my head fall back in a full belly laugh.

"Jacob, don't be silly." He steps back and can't seem to pull his eyes away.

"Seriously, you're like a siren, beautiful, sexy. So bold, not your normal conservative self. Like from a fantasy, a mermaid with legs." He babbles, and I can't help but see his face flush.

"I can change if you don't feel it is appropriate?" His head shakes frantically, denying my offer.

"No, I just wasn't expecting it. Fuck Danielle, I have always known how beautiful you are, but you're fucking hot." I feel my face heat under his lust-filled stare.

"Stop fucking with me. Let's go. We'll be late." I turn and walk towards the door.

"I'm glad this is a gay wedding, or I'd be beating the guys off with a stick. I'd go as far as tossing them over the side of the boat," he says as the door closes behind us.

"Stop playing." With my overnight bag in hand, we descend the stairs and make our way to the parking lot. "We'll take my car. I'd hate for Cherry Pie (my nickname for the Packard he bought) to be left in the lot overnight." I toss him the keys, he throws our bags in, and we settle in for the half-hour drive to the waterfront in Bayonne.

As we pull up into a spot, he places the overnight parking ticket on the dashboard, glances out the window, and sighs.

"They're here already." As a black black-tinted, out limousine pulls right in front, I turn and observe the lot. He pulls a flask from his front breast pocket and takes a swig of whatever's in it.

"You alright?" I ask, knowing he is not looking forward to seeing his parents.

He takes hold of my hand after replacing the flask. "I will be because I have you." I pat the back of his hand with my other, "you always have, always will." He nods and exits the vehicle, rounding the front to open my door like the gentleman he is.

Chapter Eight

THE CAPTAIN GREETS us as the ushers lead the way to the open-air top deck. They explain the cocktail hour will immediately follow on the second deck. The formal sit-down dinner will be in the enclosed dining room with floor-to-ceiling windows. We'll have a clear view of the city.

Jacob nervously scans the small crowd until his eyes land towards the front.

"Of course, they would take a front-row seat. They are the rudest." He reaches in his front jacket again, and I shake my head, taking a seat towards the back in the corner. This is Jonathan's and Michael's day. Whatever the conflict is between Jacob and his parents, it needs to be put on hold for today.

After about twenty minutes, the officiant makes his way to the front of the deck. The music starts as Jonathan and Michael enter from opposite sides, joining hands when they reach each other in the middle.

With kind words and best wishes, the officiant pronounces them Husband and Husband, and they kiss. I jump up from my chair, clapping with tears of joy in my eyes. Jacob whistles and the happy couple faces the small crowd and raises their joined hands. The Statue of Liberty smiles behind them. We patiently wait for them to make their way down the aisle. When they reach our row, we congratulate them both. The Captain then announces for the family and friends to retreat to the deck below to enjoy cocktail hour while the happy couple has photos taken.

"I'm so happy for them," Jacob says as we are greeted by the waitresses and waiters roaming an open-air area. Hors d'oeuvres and open bar, perfect as the sun sets and our night out begins.

"Here, you should eat," I pluck a pig in a blanket from the tray which passes by and shoves it into Jacob's mouth. He steps back laughing and bumps into no other than his father.

"You always were disrespectful in public," the older version of Jacob snarls. I step between them, "Mr. Reynolds, it's always a pleasure to see you. Excuse us. It was my fault." I try to defuse the situation before it escalates. By the look on Jacob's face, he's ready to throw down with the old man. I will not let this happen, not today.

"You're no better." The spiteful man mumbles in my direction. Without thinking, I spit out, "And yet, I am better than you." I square off with the rude old man, daring him to say something else. Jacob moves to my side, and instinctively I bring this whole disruption to an end.

I turn to Jacob and place both hands on his face, "Not now. There is a time and place, and he is not worth it, okay?" His gaze travels behind me as the Captain walks by to make sure there isn't a problem. "You ever disrespect her again, and I promise it will be the last," he says through clenched teeth.

I guide us to the other side, as far away from Mr. Reynolds as possible, with my hand in his. When we make it to the bar,

I place an order, "two tequilas, and keep them coming." He smiles as he places the lemons and salt to one side, then lines up four shot glasses and pours.

"You better keep her close," the bartender suggests to Jacob, who pulls me over by my hip. "Don't I know it." He holds up a beer in salute, and we walk the room avoiding his parents at all costs.

We overhear that not all guests are staying overnight due to availability. Let's hope his parents are part of that group. A few hors 'd'oeuvres and drinks later, the glass doors open, leading us into the dining area. The evening sky is dark, and the city lights are a beautiful backdrop.

The DJ asks that we take our seats and enjoy our meal as Jonathan and Michael have their first dance as a married couple.

Jacob excuses himself to use the restroom, "can you grab me a drink on the way back?" He smiles and nods. With my fork in hand, I cut into the filet mignon, medium-rare and delicious. I let out a moan, "Damn girl, looking that good in that dress, you shouldn't be making those sounds in public," Jacob says, placing the glasses on the table. I pull my napkin to my lips, embarrassed. I glance around the table, feeling grateful that I didn't make anyone uncomfortable.

Two gentlemen continue to glance at my cleavage as their dates, wives, or whatever they are, elbow them and then scold them loud enough to draw attention.

"Told you, you were going to cause trouble. That dress is killer. It's Nicki's, right?" he leans over, whispering. I giggle, "How'd you know?" His eyebrow raises as if I really had to ask.

"Cause it's not you, don't get me wrong, you look beautiful, fucking hot actually." His finger lines the fabric of the halter top. Following it along my neckline. I feel the heat rise from within.

"Drunk already?" I lean out from his touch, and he retreats. The music is pumping, and the colored strobe lights fill the room. I feel the need to move. I stand, grab his hand, "come on. Let's have some fun." He follows as we make our way onto the small dance floor.

Hands up in the air, and we are shaking our asses off between drinks. Over time, less people came to the dance floor. The night starts to slow down as Just the Way You Are by Billy Joel filters through the speakers. He pulls me in, and I wrap my arm around his back. We fit perfectly. It feels so right. He sings along and tilts his head slightly a few times to kiss my cheek as if the words to the song are meant for me.

I know we've been drinking, but maybe. I pull back slightly, and our eyes meet, and we both sing: "I love you just the way you are." as the saxophone finishes out the song, our lips touch. I open slightly, and he follows suit. Our tongues massage each other while our hands roam.

"Get a room!" We hear Michael call out from across the outer deck. Jacob steps back, wobbles slightly, pulls a key from his front pocket, and yells back, "we've got one!" My eyes go wide, that's right! We do!!

Without hesitation, I lean down and remove my heels. With a quick swipe, I grab the key from his hand and take off running.

"Hey! Danielle, Dani, wait up!" He slurs as he tries to catch up.

Breathless, excited, and thinking I have waited years for this, I insert the card, and the light turns green. I push the handle down, and the door opens just as Jacob spins me around and pins me against it with another amazing kiss.

One night, it's all I want. We can blame the alcohol, the atmosphere. I don't care what excuse we use. I just want one night.

Working our way inside, the kiss starts to intensify, "I have loved you forever. I can't wait to be inside you." The words send shivers down my spine. I don't say anything. I just enjoy the moment. The way he slowly unzips the back of my dress, his tender touch against my neck as he lifts the halter top to expose my breast.

"Oh, these fucking tits. They are begging for attention." He leans down and takes a nipple in his mouth, sucking, licking, and drags his teeth along my collar bone. My back arches, and I let out a moan.

"Fucking hell Dani, I need you," he says as he lays me back onto the bed.

"Jacob, I'm yours. Always have been," I whisper, pulling him to me. This is a dream, a dream come true.

Chapter Nine

Jacob

THE HORN BELLOWS THROUGH the air as I grab my head. A hangover from hell. What the fuck did I do last night? I glance around the room, recalling the wedding, my father, and dancing with Dani.

Then I remember the dream. It was so good, even better than the last few I've had. It felt real as I adjusted my boxers and made my way into the bathroom. They have been coming more frequently lately, but last night was different. It felt so right, so real. But I would never jeopardize our friendship. She means too much to me to fuck it up.

I hear the room door open, "Jacob? You okay?" She asks when I step out of the bathroom.

"Yeah, I'll be alright once I eat something." I run my hand through my hair. She's already dressed in a sundress and wedge sandals. She reaches out and hands me a coffee.

"You are the best. What would I do without you?" I sip and appreciate the aroma.

"I think maybe we should talk before the brunch," she says, and I really don't even want to go to the damn thing. With this headache from hell and my stomach-turning. How much did I drink? I find my way to the side of the bed and grab my jacket from the floor.

Yup, just as I thought, two empty flasks don't even include all the shots and drinks we had during the cocktail hour and reception. Regret tugs in my chest. I glance over to Dani.

"I didn't do anything stupid last night, did I? I know we drank a lot and danced, but I don't remember much else. I didn't puke, did I? Or say something rude or ruin Jonathan or Michael's time?"

Her face drops as if I said something wrong. "What? I didn't embarrass you, did I? Dani, if I did anything to upset you or get you mad...I...I didn't mean it. The tequila kicked my ass." I run my hand over my face. What the hell could I have done to make her look at me like that?

"Dani, I'm sorry."

* * *

Danielle

He doesn't remember. My chest tightens to the point it hurts. Unsure how he couldn't remember, I stumble in disbelief, staring wide-eyed. "Dani, please. You're my best friend. I'm sorry if I did anything to piss you off."

I step back, "no, it's just." I begin, not knowing what to say. I move to the side of the bed and throw the few things into the overnight bag I bought. The anger is feeling stronger to the point I'm pissed and unsure how to handle the situation. I want to lash out. I want to scream. Fuck! I want to hit him so hard right now.

"Dani?" I won't dare face him for fear I may do something I will regret later. I guess it's a little late for that, especially after the amazing night we spent together. Searching my brain for the fastest way to get away from him, I opened my mouth, "I was thinking maybe we could just go home and not go to brunch."

I zipper the bag shut and avoid eye contact. "I mean, your parents will be there, and you are in no condition to deal with anyone, especially them." I made up the excuse. When I woke up this morning in his arms, I thought things could be different, better. But now, I can't even bear to be in the same room with him.

"If that's what you want, it sounds good to me. Give me a few minutes, and we're out of here." He says and grabs his jeans to dress.

"I'll meet you up on deck to say our goodbyes," I tell him, throwing my bag over my shoulder and walking briskly to the door. Without another word, I let it close behind me, hiding the tears which are ready to fall.

How does someone spend one night making love to someone and not remembering? My sore body comes alive, thinking of how his hands felt against my bare skin, how his lips mapped out every inch of my body. How he told me over and over how much he loves me.

With the boat docked and the cool breeze blowing, I try to think of anything else to help clear my head. I can see my car from where I stand and wish he was staying elsewhere.

My head lifts as I wipe the last of my tears away, masking them with sunglasses. Jacob walks up behind "ready, bestie?" he asks, and I nod. We find Jonathan and Michael drinking mimosa on the upper deck. We congratulate them again and walk from the dock to the car in silence.

After the bags are in the trunk, I get in and glare out the window while he drives.

"You okay, Dani?" he tries to get me to look at him, but I can't.

"Yeah, I'm good. Just tired." I sigh.

"Thank you for coming with me. I know it was just one night, but I hope you had fun." He says, and I think, yes, it was amazing in my head. Our one night together, I will cherish and hold it dear to my heart. Yet you don't even remember. My eyes fill with unshed tears as they close.

On the way back to the apartment, he stopped for sandwiches. While he sat down to eat, I excused myself to take a shower. I wanted to wash away the feelings he brought out of me. I wanted to forget as easily as he did. Once the water turned cold, I shut it off, wrapped myself in a towel, and walked to get a bottle of water from the fridge. On the table is his sandwich wrapper, along with a note.

I had to run out. See ya later.

I'm grateful he's gone. I need time to process. I can't believe I slept with him. I can't believe he doesn't remember. Like what the fuck!?

I grab my cell and text Nicki and Keni:

Sister night, Thursday. Bring Booze. Don't tell anyone.

I know she is off on Thursday, and Diesel has Jacob working during the week, so he won't be here.

They both respond with smiley emojis. God, I love my sisters.

Chapter Ten

AFTER ANOTHER BORING week and a follow-up with my doctor, she confirmed there was a lump, and I scheduled my test. I've already spoken with mom and expected my call in regards to the test results. I guess it's time I let my sisters in on my secret. You see, breast cancer runs in my family. Prior to having my physical, I asked mom to feel in my armpit. There was something there. Just not sure if it was normal or not. So when I went for the physical, I had my doctor check, and she agreed. But she had me come back to follow up to see if it went away. Well, it didn't.

I'm on my way to pick up dinner. My sisters will meet me in a half-hour with the liquor. I am nervous yet anxious to tell them, not just about the lump but about last weekend. Talking about it is probably the best thing I can do. It's been eating me up. I've been snapping and avoiding Jacob as if he had covid or the plague. When he'd come home, I'd go out or go to my room. Avoiding him at all costs.

I pull the glass door open with a yank and step into Coliseum Pizza, the best pizza on Cedar Lane. Once I tell the kid behind the counter my name, he brings over the two large pies, one with pepperoni, the other plain, and a chicken Caesar salad. The order is paid for with a swipe, and I'm out the door. One more stop then home.

I pull up to my apartment, and Keni is waiting in the parking lot. Perfect, she can help carry the food. She opens the door, and her head snaps back, "Oh shit, this is big. Pizza, Chinese, and booze. What the fuck, Dani?" he says as she walks over to the passenger seat.

I roll my eyes, slam the driver's side door, and round the car. "Get inside, Keni, and don't plan on going home tonight." She laughs as she pulls out her phone and texts mom that she'll be late.

Bang, bang, bang. A knock at the door, "I got it," Keni says as I arrange the food on the kitchen counter and stove for easy access.

"It's big, whatever it is. It's really big." I overhear Keni tell Nicki. "What do you mean?" she replies as she crosses the doorway to the kitchen.

"Oh fuck!" she lets out, noticing all the food. She puts the box of bottles and the case of Twisted Teas on the table. As she turns and pulls me into a hug, Keni joins, and I let all my emotions pour out.

I'm a blubbering mess by the time they let me go. I look at the food as they put the alcohol in the fridge.

"Give me a shot. I'm taking a pie into the living room." I grab the roll of paper towels to use as napkins and place them and the pizza box on the coffee table. I run into my room to grab the tie hanging in my closet, and I walk to the front door, placing it on the doorknob. I retreat to the couch and crisscross my legs as I sit.

Nicki and Keni join me around the coffee table. Nicki places the bottle of Fireball to the side. I grab it immediately.

"Um, Dani. Are you okay? I've never seen you..." Nicki places an opened tea with a glass of ice in front of me as I take a big gulp, wipe my mouth with the back of my hand and slam the bottle on the table.

"I have a lump," I let out in a huff. Both of them step back in surprise. "Danielle, what did you just say?" Nicki asked. I repeated, "I have a lump in my left armpit." They both step over, and we embrace. I cried, holding them for as long as they would let me.

Once I was capable of talking again, we sat down, and I continued. "I have to have a mammogram and ultrasound, but there is definitely something there."

"I'm so sorry," Keni says, taking a seat on the floor. "We all know how hard it was for mom to see Aunt Tilly go through it, but she is still with us. One of the strongest women we know. And everyone always says how much you and she are alike. If it is, you'll fight it." She claims a slice of pepperoni.

Nicki leans back, "No, we'll fight it. Johnson Sisters kick ass together, never alone," she says and takes a sip from the bottle. She passes it to Keni, who hands it right over to me, "I love you guys, but that's not all I have to tell you." I take my sip and place the bottle on the table.

"For fucks sake, Dani, you're just full of bad news today. Can we drink a little first?" She opens a beer and hands one to Keni with a giggle.

A little while later, after we listened to Keni talk about her sexy professor and Nicki about her flavor of the week,

I grabbed a few empty cans and bottles off the table and stumbled towards the kitchen garbage can.

I pass them their drinks with refills in hand and sit back down. "Okay, now let's get back to you," Nicki hands me the fireball. I take a big gulp and let out another huff.

"I slept with him," I glance across the table. They both look at each other and squeal with excitement.

"No, no, no. It's not a good thing!" I stand, throwing my hands in the air.

Nicki grabs an eggroll and takes a bite, "this is gonna be good. It's about fucking time. Start from the beginning."

Keni sits up straight and holds up one hand, "but not TMI, no details." She takes a sip of her drink.

"You guys, this is so fucked up! You don't even know." I pace the living room and start at the beginning.

"You know we went to the wedding last weekend." Keni interrupts, "weddings always bring the lovey-dovey out of people. Why is that?" I shrug my shoulders.

"Well, anyway, Jacob was drinking before we even left here. I know he was not looking forward to seeing his parents. But this was a special day for his cousin, so I tried to keep him under control until I couldn't." I pull my hair back and throw it over my shoulder. "Your dress is at the cleaners," With a look at Nicki, she nods a thank you.

"By the end of the night, we both had way too many shots in us. Him more than me, but I was good. Not okay to drive, but I knew what I was doing. We were dancing to "Just the Way You Are" by Billy Joel, and suddenly we kissed." My hands cover my eyes, not wanting to relive the most amazing kiss I've ever experienced. After a few deep breaths, I dropped my arms, plopped down on the couch, and drank half my glass of Twisted Tea, "Anyway, it was beautiful and perfect, and I wanted more."

Nicki moves up and rubs her hand together, "now, we're getting to the good shit." Little do they know, by the time I am done telling this story, they'll want to kill the man I love and one they feel is a big brother.

"Let's drink. You'll want to be three sheets to the wind before I go any further. Cause you are not going to believe me." I take a break, trying to figure out how I'm going to tell them the rest. It's not their issue. It's mine.

"Don't tell me he's gay?" Keni asks, "Why are all the hot guys gay?" I shake my head. "No, he is not, I told you- we did the dirty, had sex, his mouth was on every inch of my body." I exclaim, and her hands cover her ears as she screams, "TMI-Dani, come on!" Nicki and I fall out into an all-out belly laugh. Nicki being the great bartender she is, pours another round. Drinking is our priority right now.

While the chit-chat goes back and forth, I check the time. Shit, Jacob should be home in an hour. I run to the front door, open it and make sure the tie is still there. Fuck him. Tonight I don't want to see him. He can find somewhere else to stay.

With giggles and another drink, I find the courage because who gives a fuck now? I'm feeling no pain.

"Okay, okay- I'm ready." They both get silent and look in my direction. "So, after we kissed, we were reminded we have a room." I sip and put the bottle on the table.

"Ah, yeah! Big sis isn't playing. She's gonna do the dirty." Nicki giggles as Keni nods.

"So anyway, we took off to the room, and let's just say. We didn't stop. We didn't question anything. It was pure. It was sexual, it was..."

Nicki stands, "Let's talk about sexy baby. Let's talk about you and me." I chuckle at the WHAM song reference. Then she adds, "you can't stop now!"

Controlling my laughter, "It was perfect. He did everything right. Until he didn't." That got their attention.

Keni sits straight up, "if that motherfucker hurt you or forced you-" I raise my hand, stopping her thoughts. "No, nothing like that. It's just..." I begin to cry, letting all my emotions out on display.

Nicki pours us another round, "When I woke up in the morning, he was wrapped around me. It felt so right. Without waking him, I figured he'd need coffee, so I got dressed and went to find some. When I returned, he was awake." I pause, wipe my face then take a big swig.

"Go on, what happened?" They both ask. I swallow hard and continue.

"He doesn't remember. He came out of the bathroom asking if he made a fool of himself and apologizing that he doesn't remember anything after dancing."

I slouch back against the couch. Both sisters come and sit on either side of me, wrapping me in their arms. Once I'm settled, Nicki stands up.

"I'm gonna kill him." Keni joins her, and suddenly I want to beat the shit out of him too.

Beer balls are in full force, "Keni calls an Uber. Dani, Go into your room and put your black jeans and blouse on. We're going out."

The room fills with giggles. She starts clapping her hands, "chop. Chop, ladies, the clock is ticking."

Chapter Eleven

Jacob

I CAME HOME, THE BAR was dead, and Diesel let me go early. I did not expect to see a tie hanging from our front door. I could feel the heat rising, the jealousy eating away at my insides as I made my way back across the courtyard. She is out and about all week, ignoring me when I am there, and now this?

With my phone in hand, I call and ask Diesel if I could hang out at his place. I honestly have nowhere else to go. Of course, there is no problem being the kind and good friend he is. When I get back to the bar to grab his keys, I run in and demand a drink.

"What the fuck Jacob? Why are you in such a pissy mood?" Diesel asks placing a beer on the coaster and his apartment keys next to it.

"There is a tie hanging on the doorknob." I grab the beer and down it.

"Yeah, so?" He asks and then steps back. "Well, I'll be damned. It's about time you admitted to yourself you have feelings for her." Shocked, I lean back and run my fingers through my hair. Has it been that obvious?

The music is playing, and Billy Joel's words have me turning on the stool. I stand and walk over to the jukebox. Dreams? No, memories fill my head.

The way we kissed on the dance floor, running down the hallway catching her at the doorway. The moment her dress hit the floor. The way she reached out for me and pulled me down. The moment I came inside her.

"Fuck!!!" I scream out. It wasn't a dream. It happened, we had one night, and we took advantage of it. We made love as if our lives depended on it, and then the next morning, I thought it was a dream.

No wonder she turned so cold, no wonder she's been avoiding me. Oh god, I fucked up big time. Panic tightens my chest as I rub it with my palm and return to the bar where Diesel stands.

"I'm going to need a shot-something stronger." I place both palms on the bar pulling in a few deep breaths.

How could I be such a dick?

* * *

Danielle

The Uber arrives, and we all pile in. "Wig Wam, on Cedar Lane, please," Nicki says, and the driver nods, puts the car in drive, and pulls away from the curb.

"We will drink and dance and laugh, no more being upset," Keni and I agree. "I got about an hour, and I gotta get home, school tomorrow. These summer classes are kicking my ass. But at least I'll graduate sooner than later. And the Professor is nice on the eyes," she says, buckling her seatbelt.

Nicki is on her cell phone, "Hold his ass there, D. I don't give a fuck if you want to live until morning, do what I say." My eyes go wide. It's common for her to speak her mind, but I thought things might have been different for her and Diesel. Guess not.

As we approach the entrance to the bar, I know tonight is going to end with one of us in jail. "Maybe we should go back or go to Buddy's or the 101?"

Nicki slides her arm through mine, "we are here. We got your back."

We step inside, and I immediately head for a back booth, not even looking to see who is here. Keni and I sit while Nicki goes to get the drinks.

There is some commotion at the bar, and I make my way to the end of the pony wall to see what's going on.

"I know I fucked up, Nicki. Give me a fucking break." Diesel says. Not wanting to come between them, I stay back, making sure she is okay.

"You let him go. I want him. Diesel, I need to talk to him." She says, slamming her fist against the bar. I have no clue what is going on. I thought she liked Diesel like she really liked him. Yeah, I know she gets around, but I see the way she acts with him. It's different.

"He's a mess. Shit hit the fan tonight. You don't even know." He continues wiping a glass out with a bar towel. "Yeah, I know more than you think, and that mother fucker owes her," she shouts, waving her hands around.

"He didn't remember, but he does now. He feels awful." I gasp at the knowledge. Nicki continues, she's looking for a fight, "he should. He's a fucking asshole. All these years, he's been pining over her, and the one time she gives in to her own feelings, he doesn't even remember. Ugh, I want to hit him so hard right now." She says, taking Diesel's beer and chugging it back.

"Not for nothing, Nicki, so what if Jacob made a mistake? She was with someone tonight. I let him duck out early. He came back because she had a tie on the door, so two wrongs don't make a right." The beer spits from her mouth as she bursts out laughing.

"Fuck face," she says, wiping her chin with the napkin, "Where do you think Keni and I have been? At her house with her, we were at the apartment drinking when she told us what had happened. She's been with us all night. I brought her here, figuring he'd be here so they can sort this shit out." She pulls her hair back, notices me in the corner, and excuses herself.

"What was that about?" I ask as she approaches, pretending not to have heard every single word.

"Nothing, let's play some darts." She waves Keni over, and we start a game. I glance at the bar and confirm Jacob isn't here. Then where is he?

Fuck him. I did what I needed to do. I got it off my chest. Now, I need to pick up the pieces and move on. Besties, that's what we are, and that's what we'll stay. Nothing more.

Chapter Twelve

Jacob

HOW COULD I HAVE BEEN so blind? How could I have thought it was a dream? The emotions of our one night together kept me from sleeping. Diesel's text claims she was at the bar with her sisters. I contemplate leaving his apartment and going home. Huh, home? Or do I go and talk to her? Or should I... an idea comes to mind, and I call the Johnson family home.

"Hi David, I know it's late. But are you up?" He says he was making his evening tea, "great, I'll see you soon." I hang up and take my keys from the front table by the door. In a rush, I quicken my steps and get into the car. Within ten minutes, I'm across town and parked outside the house.

Glaring at the front door. Debating. I take a deep breath, turn the car off and walk up the sidewalk which leads to the front door. All the while admiring the postage-stamp-sized yard, edged with flowers and the perfectly mowed lawn. This is what I want, a woman who adores me, a house I can manage, and a family.

I pull open the screen door with a deep breath and let myself in as I have done so many times before. "What's the problem, Jacob? You look lost." David greets me as I enter the kitchen.

"David, I love you like a father, and I have to tell you something." Julie joins us at the table.

She takes a seat, "this sounds important. Are you alright?" They both glances in my direction, and I pace the small kitchen.

"You're making me nervous, out with it," David spits out and leans back in his chair, intertwining his fingers and resting them on his belly.

I stop where I stand, "I love Danielle." It comes out with no hesitation, no fear, pure and honest. They glance at one another and, in unison, say, "we know," and laugh.

Dumbfounded, I stand there with my mouth open. "What? Who? How could you?" Discombobulated, I take a seat at the table and lean down at it.

"You've loved each other for years. We were just waiting for you both to grow up and realize it." Julie says while taking my hand in hers. I'm still in shock that I even said it out loud, but more so because everyone else knew without saying a word.

"Now, what are you going to do about it?" David asks, "Don't think, just blurt it out."

I look up and right into his eyes, "I'm going to marry her if she'll have me. With your blessing, of course?"

"Those are big balls you got there. It's why I like you, and we get along. I'd be honored to have you officially in our family."

They both nod, "we already consider you our son. This would just make it legal," Julie adds.

"Now, if I can convince Dani," I say, helpless, leaning back in the chair.

"You'll figure it out, and when the time is right, you'll know," Julie says. I excuse myself, stop to kiss Julie on the cheek, and shake David's hand. "Thank you. Thank you both." I'm outside in a few short strides, glancing up at the stars.

$$* * *$$

Danielle

"Hey, D!- One more round!" I hold up my shot glass and yell across the bar to Diesel. I'm so drunk I can't even see if he is there.

"I think we gotta go," Nicki takes the glass from my hand as I plop down into the booth.

"But I don't wanna," I pout. Home is where Jacob will be.

"Then come home with one of us, but you are done drinking your sorrows away. It's not the answer." Keni says she may be the youngest, but she has become the most reliable. Except for special occasions, like her birthday.

Nicki stands and reaches her arm out to help, "Come on, Dani, and tomorrow is going to suck for you."

I push my hair back from my face, "I know, and I have to go get my boobs squished," I remind myself, glancing at my phone to see the time.

Diesel comes over, "You guys need help getting home?"

Nicki rolls her eyes, "No, I called an Uber, and it should be here." He steps back as we sway our way through the bar and out the front door.

The hot, humid air suffocates me, and I take a few steps. Reaching out for the telephone pole, I bend over and puke.

I'm not sure how much time passes before I can stand up straight again.

"Are you good now?" Keni asks. I barely raise my arm but wave my hand back and forth.

"If she is puking, she is not getting in my car." The driver says, rushing back to the driver's side door, gets in, and slams the door. The locks click, so we can't get in.

"Fuck you! Asshole, this is part of your job." Nicki yells, and Keni joins the argument. I can't deal with this shit. I start walking down Cedar Lane. I need to get home and climb into bed. If I make it to Teaneck Road, make a right, and keep walking, eventually, I'll get there.

I'm not sure how long I was walking when I suddenly heard screaming from behind me.

"It's your fault, asshole. How could you do this to her?" I stop and turn around, a little more sober from all the walking.

When I figure out my surroundings, I realize I'm about halfway home. Maybe I haven't walked as far as I thought?

Keni walks up, "are you okay? We've been following you. Figured you needed some time for yourself." Nicki is arguing with Jacob in the far corner. He climbs from the car and gets in her face. Oh, fuck no!

I take off as fast as I can and go straight for him.

"Don't you get all up in her face," I yell, grabbing his shoulder and spinning him around right into a right hook. He stumbles back. I look to Nicki to make sure she's okay.

"Dani, I'm fine. He would never hurt me. It was me. I was yelling at him." She rambles off quickly, helping him stabilize.

"Well, I don't give a fuck. You fuck with one Johnson sister. You fuck with us all. Go home, Jacob." I point back to his car. I can't deal with him right now. I won't.

He retreats, holding his cheek, his eyes wide with disbelief. "You fucking hit me," he curses. The anger resonates off him. "After everything, we have been through, are you willing to throw it all away?" I turn to walk away, "just go, Jacob," the tears begin to build. There is a small commotion behind me, then I hear the car door close and the car pull away.

"Damn Dani, you sucker-punched him." Nicki starts laughing, and we all can't help but join her. We sit on the corner curb and just laugh. My laughter soon becomes tears.

"Yeah, well. It was payback. He sucker-punched my heart." Everyone's attention is on me, and I'm done having a pity party. I stand, dust my jeans off and start walking again.

"Come on, girls, I have that damn test tomorrow. I need to get some sleep." With that, Diesel pulls up, "get in the car, girls," he says, flexing. "Thanks, D," Nicki leans over and kisses his cheek.

"He's staying by me for a few days." Diesel says, with a glance through the rearview mirror, "Nice hit, by the way, Dani." I feel my cheeks flush, "well, don't fuck with a Johnson girl." I state, lean back, and look out the side window until I get home.

I jog up the stairs, across the courtyard, and into my building with a quick thanks. I don't even bother to undress. It doesn't take long before I'm fast asleep. Or maybe after all my emotions and alcohol, I pass out. Either way, my sisters had my back and got me home safely.

Chapter Thirteen

"WELCOME TO THE IMAGING center. Your name?" The woman at the front desk greets me as I approach the counter. I push the sanitizer dispenser, and it squirts out onto my hands. I rub it in, "Danielle Johnson, I have an eleven-thirty appointment." She checks her computer and then grabs a clipboard and pen.

"Fill these in, sign, and return them to me when you're done." I take the board and find a seat in the corner.

It's the normal doctor's office form until I get to the last one.

The reason for my visit: I check the prescription and write what it says. Mammogram with ultrasound diagnosis N63 stands for an unspecified lump in the breast, and the code R22.2 is for localized swelling mass and lump.

As I sign the last form, I think about my aunt and how devastating it was to hear a few years back when she discovered she had breast cancer, and like the warrior she is, she took charge and is still with us today, cancer-free.

With a deep breath, I place the clipboard on the counter and retake my seat, hoping that if this turns out to be positive, I have the strength to fight it and live a long and happy life.

Why do most doctor's offices have fish tanks? I think as I watch the angelfish swim back and forth.

"Danielle Johnson?" I glance up and stand. "Follow me, please," the nurse says. We walk around the corner and down a hall. "If you can step inside, remove everything from your waist up and put the gown on with the opening to the front." I nod, acknowledging her instructions.

A few moments later, I stepped out of the dressing room and was escorted to the room. I chuckle to myself when I see the machine with the plastic attachments and think of my mother saying, "they flatten them things out like a pancake."

The nurse comes over and asks me to expose myself, "Are you at least going to buy me dinner first?" She giggles but, trying to be professional, clears her throat. She reached out, placing these Band-Aid-looking markers under my left armpit, where the doctor felt the lump and one over each nipple. Talk about weird things.

After a few other instructions, and deep breaths, I can confirm: they really do flatten them like pancakes, it's not that it hurts, but it is very uncomfortable. The way the machine holds one boob while you stand squared off with a machine, slightly turned yet facing forward. As the nurse steps on the pedal, a thick arm comes down, and it makes contact with your breast and squishes! Pancake.

"Hold still and take a deep breath," she walks away, presses a button, and the machine takes its images.

"Okay, one more side to go. Are you okay?" I nod, just wanting it to be over.

Once she is done positioning me the way she needs for the best image results, the machine releases my breast, and I step back. My arm slides back into the gown, and I hold it closed while we step out of the room and down another hall into a private waiting area where a different technician stands holding a folder.

"Danielle Johnson?" I nod, following her into what I assume is the ultrasound room. I take a seat on the bed, "Please lie down, open the gown and pull out your left arm, please," she instructs.

"You get to fondle my goods without even taking me for dinner. No flowers or nothing, huh?" She shakes her head with a smile. The bottle of the gel makes a farting sound as it squishes out onto my breast. It takes about five minutes of her moving this magic wand around under my left breast. Then she concentrates on the arm-pit area. I watch as she stares at the screen, clicking, typing, and coding whatever it is she sees. Once she seems satisfied, she tells me I can use the gown to remove the excess gel and get dressed, but not to leave just yet.

With the gown in hand, I remove the gel and toss it into the bin labeled laundry. I remove the markers and put my bra and shirt back on with a quick yank.

My legs hang from the side of the bed, swaying back and forth while I wait patiently. About ten minutes go by when the door opens, and a doctor comes in.

"Hi Miss. Johnson, I'm Dr. Gordon. I'm an oncologist." He takes the short round chair, rolls it to the side of the bed, and sits.

"Hi, you can call me Dani," I say and reach out my hand to shake his.

"Thank you, Danielle. As you know, you are here because your primary doctor felt something during your physical. The good news is, she was right. Whatever it is, it's small. The bad news is, we won't know more without a biopsy." He pulls the monitor over and uses his pen to show me on the screen.

Not wanting to believe this is cancer, I gulp down the shock and take a few deep breaths.

"When? How soon can we schedule this?" He checks his appointment book on the computer to the left and turns back in my direction. "Next week, Tuesday at eight-thirty a.m."

I agree and take the card with the time, date, and location as I walk mindlessly through the halls, past the reception area, and out to my car.

Once I get inside, the tears begin to fall before I can even put my keys in the ignition.

This can't be happening. I'm only twenty-six, for fucks sake. If it's cancer, I'll probably have to do Chemo. I could lose my hair, my boobs. Fuck that- I could lose my life!

With my face resting in my palms, I cry uncontrollably. I'm not sure how much time passed before I calmed down enough to drive. I grab a tissue from the box on the floor and blow my nose, and with another, wipe the tear stains from my cheeks.

All I can think about is wanting my mommy. As soon as I'm stable, I start the car and pull out my phone. I sent a quick text to Keni and Nicki, asking them to meet me at our family home. They quickly respond. I'm sure they have been waiting to hear from me.

I drive across town, and I'm parked in my parent's driveway before I know it. Pulling the lever, I open the car door, feeling numb, but I make my way up the short path.

I turned the doorknob with a shaky hand and walked in the front door. The look on my face told my mother the news.

She rushed down the hall and took me into her arms. "I'm so sorry, mom," I cry. She hushed me and rubbed my back while saying, "this is not something someone can control. I'm sorry the gene runs in our family. But it's not confirmed yet. This could be nothing."

She takes hold of my arms and pulls back, looking into my face. "Whatever it is, you are not alone. We all love you and will be with you every step." I hug her again, and we walk back into the kitchen. I excuse myself to use the bathroom while Mom updates Dad.

When I open the door to exit, he is there with open arms. "Daddy," I gasp and see Keni standing to the side, waiting for her turn. After a moment, he released, and she wasted no time filling the gap between us. "Hey, hey." I feel her tears through the cotton of my shirt.

"I got this, no worries. Okay?" I try to be brave for my little sister. I calm myself again with a few deep breaths, and we walk into the living room. Once we all settle, Nicki arrives, and I explain step by step what they did, "And mom, you were right, they squish them like a pancake." I can't help the chuckle that bubbles up from my throat and the relief I feel talking about this. I am so lucky to have a family who listens and is here for me whenever I need them, day or night.

Once everyone is over the initial shock, we agree it will stay between us. There is no reason to let any of the other family members know until we have the results.

"What about Jacob?" My father asks while leaning back in the recliner. "What about him?" I ask. "Don't you think you should tell him?" I shrug my shoulders, "No. It's none of his business." I stand from the couch and take my purse from the end table.

"He loves you, you know?" he says. "Yeah, Dad, and I love him, but I don't want to be with someone if it's out of pity. Or worse, if I'm not going to be able to grow old with him. Just don't say anything, please?" I plead with my eyes. He nods.

"I'm going home. I need to wash this day away and start fresh tomorrow." Hugs and kisses are passed out to all along with a thank you, and I leave.

Home is exactly the place where I need to be.

Chapter Fourteen

A *few weeks later...*

TUESDAY'S APPOINTMENT came and went. Afterward, I felt weak, and my shoulder was sore and stiff for a few days. There is a scar under my arm that Dr. Gordon said should fade over time. Luckily, I only get the tingling when something touches the area. Other than that, everything else seems to be healing.

It can take seven to ten days for the results to come back. Jacob keeps calling, and I keep ignoring him. He has sent flowers to my office and left more than enough long messages on my voicemail, begging me to call him back so he can explain. But he never goes into detail.

Explain what? That you fucked me and don't even remember? Ugh, every time I think about it, I get pissed off more and more.

Maybe it's the stress of the test, the waiting for the results. Or maybe I'm just done, done pining for someone who doesn't want me.

Suddenly the conversation from the night at my parent's plays in my head.

"What about Jacob?" My father asked.

"What about him?" I replied.

"Don't you think you should tell him?" He continued.

I shrugged my shoulders, "No. It's none of his business."

"He loves you. You know?" Dad said.

Does he love me?

I pull my phone from my desk and text mom.

Did dad say Jacob loves me?

The three dots appear, and the reply takes a moment to pop onto the screen

Yes, and he does.

For the last two weeks, I've been in a fog, a stress-induced coma, and I guess I wasn't paying much attention to things. I wonder how they know? I swipe and hit my mom's picture to dial her line as I lean back in my chair and face my boss's office door.

"Hi honey, how are you doing?" she answers after two rings. "I'm just in a waiting limbo. You know how I love to wait," I answer, getting up and walking over to the copy machine to retrieve the Maintenance Agreements I've printed out.

"How do you know he loves me?" I ask in a whisper. Not wanting any of my co-workers to know about my love life. She laughs, "The two of you have loved each other for years. It just wasn't your time yet." She admits.

"What makes you so sure?" I wonder about tapping the end of the pen against my lip.

"He came here. He admitted it. I don't know what got you both pissed off with each other, but work it out. You'll never love someone the way you love him. I can see it every time he walks into a room. You light up. He's it for you." I sigh in defeat. "I know, I think that's what scares me," I admit, plopping down in my office chair. "What if this test comes back positive? What if they have to remove my breast? What if I lose my hair, mom? He could never be with someone like that. He deserves better," I admit.

"Danielle, you listen to your mother. When you love someone, it doesn't matter what they look like or what changes they go through in life. You and Jacob are soul mates. You were lucky enough to find each other. The rest will fall into place." I agree to an extent. But can't you see, I don't want him to start a life together with me with all these issues. "Maybe it's not our time yet." I whisper, "Mom, I have to go. I'll talk to him after the results come back," I promise.

We talked about our weekend plans to meet up at the car show across town.

"Hey, mom, what if he is there? He mentioned registering the car to do some shows."

She answers, "I don't think he made it on time for this one. It's early in the season. Besides, if he's there, who cares? You are bound to bump into him eventually." Suddenly I feel like this could be a trap or a setup. I stay silent for a moment longer.

"I love you, Dani, anytime you need me." She states. "I love you more," I say, ending the call.

Time went a little quicker today, as I noticed the clock reached four o'clock. I turn my computer off and head out of the office. All I want to do is get home, take a shower and stop thinking about everything.

* * *

The shower was refreshing, and I felt relaxed as I slid my legs into a pair of sweatpants and tugged my t-shirt from behind the elastic. I turn into the kitchen and reach out to open the fridge and retrieve a beer. I stick a few in the freezer to get them extra cold while I pull a bag of popcorn from the cabinet and place it inside the microwave.

As the aroma fills the apartment, I grab a bowl and place it on the counter. Then enter the living room and take the remote, turning on the television. With a push of the button, I search HBO, Starz, and other movie channels for something that may entertain me.

My phone pings. It's Keni.

Keni: What's up? I'm bored.

I text back.

Me: Movie night?

She replies immediately.

Be there in fifteen.

I send a smiley face and switch back to the regular channels to see what to watch while I wait. I retrieve the popcorn, make sure I have some snacks, and wait. Seems like that's all I do lately is wait.

Wait for the results, wait for Jacob to get his head out of his ass, wait for my sisters to grow up, wait for my workday to end. Wait, wait, and wait!

A knock at the door has me up and crossing the hardwood floors. I turn the knob and yank the door open with a flick of the wrist. Standing outside is Jacob.

Stunned, I step back, "what are you doing here?" He raises his hands in a surrender motion.

"Dani, I just needed to see you. You don't have to say anything. Just let me talk." He says, and I'm not ready to hear what he has to say. Not without knowing what my test results are. Not knowing if I could offer him a future.

I stand with my hand holding the door, ready to slam it at any moment. But I don't.

"Danielle, I have loved you for as long as I can remember. I know I fucked up. It was never supposed to happen. I have too much respect for you to have done such a thing. I guess what I am trying to say is that I'm sorry. I'm sorry I dream about you all the time, and having the liquid courage, I took advantage of the situation. I honestly thought it was just another dream until about a week later. I heard the song again, and it all came rushing back to me. I guess what I am trying to say and what is most important is: I'm sorry."

He steps back to walk away, just as Keni and Nicki are walking up the walkway. They shimmy passed Jacob with a small wave and into the apartment. Once they are inside, I step out, "Jacob. I don't know what to say to that. I mean, for so long, I've waited, and now everything is a mess. All because of one drunken night... I'm confused and lost and have other things on my mind. Just give me time to figure things out." I reach for the door as my eyes fill with tears. "Dani, I'm sorry," he says, turns on his heels, and walks away.

What the fuck? What the fuck am I supposed to do with the knowledge which he just rambled. He dreams about me. He's sorry. He should never have. Like. What. The. Fuck?

I rush through the apartment and retreat to the bathroom, where I stand staring in the mirror. My blood is boiling. I can't argue with him. I can't confess to him. I can't do anything until

I know what's in store for my future. I turn the faucet on and grab the washcloth. Once I clear my mind and face, I return to the living room as if our confrontation never happened.

"Hey, I didn't know you were coming too." I reach out and embrace Nicki with a hug. "I'm glad you came," I kiss Keni on the cheek, "it's hot as fuck out there." She says, "the air is on." I notice they placed a couple of bags of chips on the coffee table, and a case of beer and tea are in the fridge.

"So, we had an idea!" Nicki claps her hands together, and I look at Keni. She is all smiles, which makes me nervous.

"Oh yeah, what's that?" I plop down on the couch.

"You know how Jacob has the Packard. I thought if we could borrow it, we could re-make the Warrant video for mom and dad's anniversary. It would be funny, and you know how much they love that shit."

Right now, with everything going on, I don't want anything to do with Jacob. The more space between us, the easier it will be if I decide not to get involved. I shy away from the thought, but she's right. They would totally enjoy and appreciate it if we went out of our way to make a video.

I start to giggle. "Only our parents would appreciate seeing their kids in red halter tops, daisy duke shorts, dancing half-naked on a car." But it would be us, and it is their favorite song, I give it some thought. Keni jumps up and down "right. They would totally love that shit!" she says.

"I'll think about it." We have a couple of weeks before the family gathering. It should take a few days or one really long day to try and shoot the video. First, we would have to find the place and get red halter tops and booty shorts. But I think it would be doable.

"So, what are we watching?" Keni asks and plops down next to me on the couch. "I'm thinking of a thriller or something scary." She grabs some popcorn and tosses it into her mouth.

Shaking my head, "I hate scary movies," she laughs at me and throws the pillow, hitting my shoulder.

"What about the foreign film 365 DNI?" Nicki recommends and takes a seat in the recliner. "I hear it's good!" Keni adds, but do I really want to watch a sex movie with my sisters?

"I just subscribed to that new streaming network, Passionflix. It's the one where they bring books to the screen. Should we check that out?" they both groan.

Nicki rolls her eyes, "you and your damn books." I throw the pillow in her direction and tell them, "I know, I know. But they have produced some great stories. But we can watch something else."

I connect my phone, so it will mirror onto the wide-screen television and pull up the Prime app.

We watched a few trailers and decided on Rock of Ages. Since we started the night talking about mom and dad and the '80s, it's perfect. Besides, we love all the music, and I can use something upbeat.

As the movie plays, we sing along to all the oldies we were raised listening to. It was a perfect time to forget everything and enjoy the night.

By midnight the movie was over, and I was exhausted. We cleaned up the little mess that was made, and I walked them to the door. With quick kisses to the cheeks, we say goodnight.

"I'll see you guys tomorrow at the car show. Love ya!." I wave, watching them walk down the stairs into the courtyard and out of sight. I close the door, lock up and turn the lights off, making my way into the bedroom.

Quickly glancing at my phone to see if Dr. Gordon had called, disappointed when he hadn't. Ugh, the wait is killing me.

Chapter Fifteen

AFTER ANOTHER RESTLESS night, I'm up at the crack of dawn. I went for a run, came home, had my coffee, and took a shower in preparation for meeting up with the family. The sun is shining. It's going to be another hot one. I slide my legs into my jean shorts and throw my tank top over my head. The phone rings, and I run into the kitchen to grab it.

Dr. Gordon's Office flashes on the screen. Nervous, and with a shaky hand, I press the green circle.

"Hello." I answered, "Good morning Miss. Johnson, this is Dr. Gordon. I know it's Saturday, but I didn't want to postpone giving you your results." I gulp down the fear as I sit down at the kitchen table.

"I appreciate you calling." It is all I can get out before the fear gets the better of me and tears start to fall down my cheeks.

"We, as doctors, are fully aware of how frustrating it is to wait on answers, and when the file was emailed to me this morning, I couldn't wait. Your results came back. They are negative."

I let out the breath I didn't even know I was holding. "It's not cancer?" the tears begin to fall. "No, he confirms." I sigh in relief, "thank you, Dr. Gordon. Thank you so much." He wishes me well and reminds me to continue to follow up, and we will treat with an antibiotic and anti-inflammatory. If it doesn't dissipate within a few weeks, they will continue to keep an eye on it.

I disconnected the call, covered my face with my hands, and thanked the Lord for the negative results. I'm not normally a praying person, but I reached out these last few weeks, and I owe whoever was listening a big thank you.

I rushed into the bathroom with a glance at my watch and washed my face. I add mascara and eyeliner with a smile staring at my reflection, and brush my hair straight.

For the first time in weeks, I feel good. The stress has diminished from being a heavy weight on my shoulders.

I slide my feet into my sneakers and grab my keys. Once the door closes behind me, I make my way down to my car and turn the engine over. I tune the station to the oldies and, sure as shit, Cherry Pie is playing. I sit listening to the words, recalling all the times Jacob has called me his Cherry Pie ever since prom night after our first kiss.

I giggle at the words:

"Swingin' on the front porch," I dance and sing along to the words. My mood is lighter now that the doctor has given me the newest that it's not cancer.

We spent all those summer nights in his backyard when no one else was home. All the times we could have, maybe should have hooked up. But we didn't. We both respected our friendship too much. I continue to listen.

"Looks so good; bring a tear to your eye."

"Swing it!" I sing along with them and throw the car in gear. I've waited long enough. We've waited long enough. I think now is our time. I'm going to throw caution to the wind and tell him how I feel, how I have always felt. I love him.

I'm healthy, and I deserve to be happy. I turn the wheel to the right, making a detour up Cedar Lane. Within two blocks, I found a parking spot across the street from the Wigwam. I slam the car into park and jump out. Glancing to the left, then right, I start running across the street, a car blares its horn, but I don't stop. This is too important.

With a yank, I swing the heavy door open into darkness. I push the curtain aside, "Diesel?" I call out, and he comes from the back room. "What's up, Dani?" He asks, placing a case on the bar he must be stocking for the day shift. "Where's Jacob?" I ask, rushing through and around, searching for him.

"Dani, calm down. What's wrong? He's not here. He went to his house, and then he's got plans this afternoon." I stop in my tracks. Am I too late? Wait.

"His house?" what does he mean he went to his house? "You've been keeping to yourself. He didn't want to stay on my couch anymore, so he went home."

Confused, I place both hands on the bar, "Diesel, he doesn't have a home. His home is with me."

Diesel steps back, "maybe you need to tell him that then." He says and walks towards the back, mumbling, "What the hell is wrong with these Johnson chicks," shaking his head, walking through the swinging doors which lead to the kitchen.

"Maybe I should," I whisper to no one in particular, staring blankly at the empty bar. I pull out my phone and start a group chat with my sisters, letting them know I'm on my way and I am okay with making the video.

With one foot in front of the other, pounding the pavement, I make my way back to my car. Once inside, I admire the photo I have set as my screensaver. The one of Jacob and me are standing proudly in front of his house before we left for prom.

I pull up his contact, press message, and type.

I'm sorry.

It's all I have to say, and I'll hope my stubborn ass is not too late to make things right with him.

The three dots appear, but no response.

"Fine. Be a stubborn asshole." I chuck my phone into the cup holder and turn the car over, blasting my favorite, Lita Ford's Kiss me Deadly song. I rock it out as I drive across town to the car show.

"Come on, pretty baby," I scream as I pull into the lot and turn the car off.

The place is packed already, and with a pep in my step. I search for my family. About five minutes go by when I see them waving from the vendor's corridor to the left of all the cars.

I walk closer, mom looks in my direction, and I run, wrapping her in my arms. "Hey, hey. What the heck, Danielle." She says, pushing me back to arm's length when she sees I'm smiling.

"Yeah!" I nod, and she wraps me tighter.

"It's negative," I say loud enough for them all to hear. Happy tears stream down, my father kisses my forehead, and we all join arm in arm and begin our tour around the classic cars.

"I'm so happy. I don't even know what to do with myself." I say giddy, knowing now I can plan a future. Maybe one with Jacob, if I haven't blown my chance.

Music is playing. Families admire the vehicles as much as we are. We stop and take photos in front of a few. When we get toward the end, I notice Keni slows down and looks nervous.

I slow down and wait for her as the others proceed. "What's up, little sister?" I place my arm over her shoulder, wondering what's got her on edge.

"Nothing," she snaps and turns her head to face away from the cars. I search to see what she is avoiding, and my eyes land on orange with a black striped muscle car. A Chevrolet Chevelle SS, nice.

The guy standing next to it talking isn't too bad either. Muscular but not ripped like Diesel or tall like Jacob. He's older than Keni. His hair, like most guys, is tight along with the ear and a little longer on top. His mustache and beard are short scruffs, well maintained or groomed if you will.

"Um, is there something I should know about, Keni?" I come right out and ask. As we walk past, I hear a male voice, "Kendra, is that you?" The man approaches, and Keni's face turns red.

"Boy, it sure is hot out here," I fan my face with my hand.

Kendra rolls her eyes and turns, "Good afternoon Professor Manning." He stops, places his hands in his jean pockets then asks, "Enjoying the show?" I step forward, "How rude of me. I'm Kendra's sister, Danielle. Nice to meet you, Professor, is it?" I shake his hand and then step back.

"Yeah, sorry, Professor, but we have to catch up with our family," she says, pulling my arm, and we dash away like little school girls giggling until we come up behind our parents. "Nicki is off doing her thing but will be back," they say.

I bump Keni's shoulder, "so when did professors get so fucking hot?" She laughs and ignores my questions.

With that, we step in front of the Packard. Turning my head left and then right, there is no sign of Jacob. Disappointment fills me.

"Disappointed?" My father asks. "A little, I guess," I admit with a shrug off my shoulders.

"Excuse me! Excuse me, can I have everyone's attention?" The surrounding speakers squeal, and everyone quickly puts their hands over their ears.

"Is that Nicolette?" My mother points while looking around to find out what's going on.

Everyone crowds around the car, mumbling to each other and wondering why they have all been called over here. Then the music begins to play, and I hear the words:

"Don't go changing...

Jacob appears from behind the tent, holding a microphone up to his mouth.

My eyes fill with tears. He's singing to me. This guy, my best friend, is going out of his comfort zone to prove his love for me.

My mom, dad, and sister step back, leaving me in the open, stunned at what I'm witnessing. Jacob gets closer, his eyes on mine as he continues to sing Billy Joel's song.

The same song from the wedding. The one night we had together, which he forgot. A tear escapes. The one night I dreamed of, and the one he claims he's been dreaming of.

It comes to an end. It's so quiet you could probably hear a pin drop.

"Danielle Johnson, I know I fucked up. But, if you'll let me, I will work every damn day for the rest of our lives to make it up to you. You are my best friend, my safe place. You've become my heartbeat, my last breath, because, without you, Dani, I'm nothing."

I swallow his words and leap forward into his arms. He has me leaning back in one swift move, kissing me as if our lives depended on it.

"I love you, Cherry Pie." He says with a kiss on my nose as he lifts me to a standing position. People all around are clapping. I'm so embarrassed I hide my face against his chest.

Along with Keni and Nicki, my parents approached and, each one in their own way, said, "it was about time."

As the day came to an end, everyone went their separate ways. I, of course, stayed by Jacob's side. He wouldn't let me go now that we were finally together.

Finally, I ask, "So you broke down and went home, huh?" His smile faltered. "Actually, my father called me and, at the time, we weren't talking, so I answered just to have someone to yell at." He chuckles, placing his elbows on his knees. I slide my arm through his giving him my undivided attention. "It turns out they were going to sell the house, and he wanted to know if I would have any interest."

I gasp, "Jacob, I love that house. Why are they selling it?" He turns and places his bottle of water on the asphalt.

"Turns out they'd rather live in the south, which is fine with me. The further away, the better. I've been staying there and cleaning out all the old stuff."

* * *

I take his hand in mine, "so you'll come back and stay with me?" He pushes my hair behind my ear, "I was kinda hoping you'd come live with me. I bought it."

I gasp, "Jacob, are you sure?" He nods, "Yes. I gave it a lot of thought, and even though childhood wasn't the greatest in that house, it wasn't all bad. I mean, it's where I met you." I lean in and kiss his cheek.

"Besides, we can fill it with a couple of kids and make a real home of it with you. Maybe even start those traditional Barbecues like my grandparents used to have. So, what do you think?"

"Jacob, nothing would make me happier." I place my arms around his neck and kiss the man I love. The boy from next door, my best friend, my soulmate.

The End...

Stay Tuned:

ONE HOUR
   One Kiss

About Elaine Marie

I'M A TRUE JERSEY GIRL at heart. I currently reside in the northern part of the beautiful Garden State—New Jersey—with my hubby, three amazing children, and our dogs and cats.

In my spare time, I can be found rooting for my favorite football and hockey teams. Other than my family, my passion is reading and creating amazing stories that captivate the heart.

Contact Elaine Marie

Facebook:

https://m.facebook.com/EMarieBooks/

Twitter:

@EMarieBooks

Instagram:

@ElaineMarieAuthor

TikTok:

@EMarieBooks

Email:

ElaineMarieAuthor@gmail.com

Books By Elaine Marie

Déjà vu[1]
Snow Kisses[2]
Sunshine Kisses[3]
Falling for the Dare The Falling Series Book 1[4]
Falling for the Past The Falling Series Book 2[5]
Living[6]
Because I Can The Because Trilogy Book 1[7]
Because I Won't The Because Trilogy Book 2[8]
TTYL The FYI < 3 Series Book 1[9]
L8R London The FYI < 3 Series Book 2[10]
WTF Venice The FYI < 3 Series Book 3[11]
OMG Cabo The FYI < 3 Series Book 4[12]

---

1. http://amzn.com/B07GDVY91W

2. http://amzn.com/B01N1RZH2I

3. https://www.amazon.com/dp/B0875M4VZP

4. http://Amzn.com/B07RB2G6S9

5. http://Amzn.com/B07RB2G6S9

6. http://amzn.com/B06XK4BWYH

7. http://amzn.com/B01LYI56O2

8. http://amzn.com/B07GC634S6

9. http://amzn.com/B07D7GFH1J

10. http://amzn.com/B07D857Y2M

11. http://amzn.com/B07GGBFGWB

12. http://amzn.com/B07HGJP83J